# Ballroom Bits

## HEDGEWITCH FOR HIRE – BOOK 9

## CHRISTINE POPE

BALLROOM BITS

Copyright © 2023 by Christine Pope

ISBN: 978-1-946435-62-0

Published by Dark Valentine Press

Cover design by Lou Harper

Formatting by Indie Author Services

## Shall We Dance?

"STOP FIDDLING WITH THAT," I TOLD MY friend Archie, who was adjusting his white bow tie for what felt like the hundredth time. Yes, the man had a wealth of Virgo placements in his astrological chart, but his current finickiness seemed a bit over the top even for him.

His mouth tightened. "This is a *very* important competition."

*Tell me something I don't know,* I thought, although I knew better than to say the words aloud. When Archie got like this, it was usually better to avoid any utterances that might result in a stern lecture as to why I was taking a particular set of circumstances much too casually.

Besides, he wasn't exactly over-inflating the situation. True, when compared to massive problems like world hunger or climate change, doing well in a regional ballroom dance competition might not have seemed like that big a deal, but Archie and his fiancée Victoria had been working toward this weekend for almost six months now, and I knew they were hoping to do well, even if Archie wasn't quite willing to admit that he had his eye on the big prize—a gold medal in the multi-dance competition at the Stepping Stars dancesport tournament.

My husband Calvin and I had accompanied Archie and Victoria to Scottsdale this Memorial Day weekend to offer moral support. Well, that was Calvin's and my stated reason for attending, although I'd be lying if I didn't also admit that the idea of spending four days away from our tiny hometown of Globe in a ritzy Scottsdale resort didn't have its own appeal.

Victoria had already headed downstairs to check in and wait backstage for the gold multi-dance competition to begin, but Archie, true to form, had deemed his tie not ready for prime time, and had continued to fuss in front of the mirror. Because I'd known him for more than two years by this point—although during the first year of Archie's and my relationship, he'd still been in cat form thanks to a curse a witch had cast on him decades earlier, thus negating the need for white tie —I realized there wasn't any point in rushing him. No, I'd told my husband I'd stay behind and hold

Archie's hand, and then go find him down in the audience once Archie was ready to join Victoria backstage.

"You're going to do great," I said, doing my best to sound encouraging without being too overtly cheery about the whole thing. Archie would have seen through any false words of support the second they left my lips. "Especially since you've had so much more room to practice in lately."

Maybe the tense set of his shoulders relaxed just the slightest bit. "True," he allowed.

After Archie had become human again, I'd offered him my old apartment over the store I owned downtown, since by that point, Calvin and I were about to be married and I was soon to move into his sprawling pueblo-style house a few miles outside Globe. After Archie met Victoria—she'd planned Calvin's and my wedding—the couple had at first used the second bedroom for a practice space, an arrangement that had worked for a while, even if the room wasn't exactly the sort of place where you could perform an extravagant Viennese waltz.

But once Archie popped the question to Victoria on this past New Year's Eve, the two of them had realized the only smart thing to do was to buy a larger property somewhere in Globe, since she'd already planned to close down her wedding planning business in Scottsdale once she'd completed her interior design certification. High-end houses weren't exactly thick on the ground in our part of the world, but my friend Josie, Globe's mayor and its most accomplished real estate agent, found the couple a place almost immediately.

Their luck in locating a more suitable nest had come about because the house had once belonged to Miriam Jacobsen, who was currently cooling her heels in the Florence Correctional Facility after being convicted of conspiracy to commit murder. Miriam's sister had been sitting on the property for ages, asking far more for it than anyone could reasonably expect to spend on a four-bedroom, three-thousand-square-foot house in our out-of-the-way town, but somehow Josie had managed to wheedle her into lowering her asking price. And because Victoria's Scottsdale condo had gone into escrow almost as soon as she put it on the market and therefore she had a down payment ready to go, the whole transaction went a lot smoother than anyone probably had any right to expect.

Anyway, Archie and Victoria's new digs had something that most homes in Globe—or Arizona itself, for that matter—didn't have, which was a huge, fully finished basement. Josie's handyman nephew Brett pulled up the old carpet and laid down hardwood, and soon enough, my friends had enough space down there to hold their own ballroom dance competition if they wanted to.

"Your tie is perfect," I told Archie, who at last had stopped fussing with the thing and was gazing at his reflection with narrowed eyes.

Did it still feel strange to see his human face staring back at him? True, he'd been himself for almost a year now, but he'd been a cat for much longer than that—seven-plus decades—so I supposed it was possible the novelty hadn't completely worn off.

If he was experiencing any cognitive dissonance, however, he definitely didn't show any signs of it. Now that the tie had stopped giving him trouble, he looked composed, chiseled features still and focused, bright blue eyes showing nothing of the tension he must have been feeling right then. His wavy dark blond hair had been combed away from his face and held in place with some pretty serious pomade, only cementing the general impression he tended to give, which was that of a Golden Age movie star who'd somehow blundered his way into the twenty-first century.

Well, Archie was definitely a man out of time, although back when he'd lived in Globe in the early 1950s, he'd been a history teacher at the local high school, not an actor. And even though Josie had tried on more than one occasion to cajole him into performing in one of her beloved Old Globe

Theatre Company's productions, he'd always declined, saying he really wasn't interested in the stage.

Why playing Mortimer Brewster in *Arsenic and Old Lace* seemed anathema to him, while he was just fine with putting on tails and dancing the foxtrot in front of hundreds of spectators, I really couldn't say. Maybe it was only that when he was dancing, he was with Victoria, and therefore the onlookers didn't matter.

As crazy as I was about my husband, I had to admit I'd never seen anyone fall for another person the way Archie had fallen in love with Victoria. True, he'd spent his entire life thinking he was asexual when he was actually demisexual—someone who only had romantic feelings for one person, and one alone—but still, his devotion to her continued to surprise me.

"Besides," I went on, "you've got a whole trunk waiting downstairs with replacement shoes and shirts and ties, so if anything happens to that one, it's not like you don't have backups."

He let out a breath but apparently decided not to contradict me...probably because he knew I was right. Calvin had helped Archie lug the thing backstage a few hours earlier, wedging it in among the other trunks and suitcases and garment bags in the area designated for storing the competitors' personal belongings.

A nod, and he said, "Well, we should head down. I don't want Victoria to think I've abandoned her."

I kind of doubted such a thought would even enter her mind—more than anyone else, she understood the depth of his attachment to her—but I didn't protest. The evening's competition wouldn't be starting for almost half an hour, and yet it was still better not to go rushing backstage at the last minute.

So I replied, "Sure," and picked up my beaded evening bag from where I'd set it down on the dresser before I headed out into the hallway. Even with the multi-dance portion of the event set to start in the next twenty-five minutes or so, plenty of people crowded the corridor—spectators like me, and men and women dressed to the nines, clearly competitors.

Actually, I'd dressed up, too, mostly because Victoria had told me that a lot of the people who attended these events looked at them as the perfect opportunity to wear that special cocktail dress or tux they had hanging in the closet. I wasn't exactly the type to have a wardrobe full of evening wear, since running a New Age shop in little Globe, Arizona, didn't require that sort of attire. However, since I also was never one to turn down a chance to go shopping if an event called for new clothes, I'd bought several cocktail dresses and one evening gown for the occasion. Calvin probably wouldn't wear a tux even if you put a gun to his head, but the suit he'd worn to our wedding worked just fine, and he didn't have any problems putting that on in order to give the competition the respect it deserved.

Because there were so many people coming and going, Archie and I had to wait about five minutes before we were finally able to catch an elevator heading down to the conference level. Several of the passengers in the elevator car gave me slightly puzzled looks, probably wondering what I was doing with one of the competitors, since my own outfit made it clear that I was here as a spectator and nothing more.

No one asked any awkward questions, though, and soon enough, the two of us were able to disembark in the lobby, then head toward the conference center where the actual dance contests were being held. This level of the resort was even more crowded—who knew so many people were into ballroom dance competitions?— but eventually Archie and I were able to thread our way through the throng and reach the back-stage area.

Since Archie had looped a lanyard with his competitor's pass around his neck just as we were leaving his hotel room, the security guard standing at the door didn't challenge us when we entered, but only gave us a brief nod and stepped out of the way.

The backstage was utter pandemonium—men and women in tails and evening gowns bustling to and fro, others dressed nicely like I was, probably there to lend moral support or act as gofers. I could see Archie's mouth compress as we made our way through the crowds and guessed he must hate this part of competitions, the chaos under the surface, even if everything appeared serene and polished once he stepped out onto the dance floor with Victoria.

Since he was at least six inches taller than I was, he had an advantage when it came to scanning through the crowd to see where his fiancée might be waiting for him. He must have spotted her, because he hastened his stride while I followed in his wake, even as I wondered whether he might physically push someone aside in order to reach her more quickly.

But no, Archie would never be that rude, even when he was in a hurry. A moment later, I saw Victoria as well, a vision in her ice-blue ballgown with an intricate beaded pattern all down the bodice and trailing across the full skirt, which was edged in ostrich feathers.

A little flamboyant for my taste, although I knew this was all part of the competition, to have a dress that sparkled and a skirt that rippled and swirled as Archie twirled her across the dance floor. So far, they'd stuck to the traditional dances—waltz, tango, foxtrot—and I knew that was because Archie just couldn't stomach the idea of putting on the sequined jumpsuit that seemed to be *de rigeur* for the men participating in the Latin dance part of the competition.

As we drew closer, I saw that Victoria wasn't alone, that a man in white tie and tails stood a little closer to her than I thought was strictly polite. Judging by the tense set of her shoulders and the artificial smile she wore, I guessed she wasn't too thrilled by the man's proximity.

Neither was Archie, whose lips thinned even further as he approached. However, his tone was pleasant enough as he said, "Hello, Brad."

Clearly, they were acquainted, probably because the group of competitive ballroom dancers in Arizona wasn't exactly what you could call large. "Hello, Archie," Brad replied, his tone clearly dismissive. His gaze slid to me for just a second, appraising, but then flicked away as soon as he caught sight of the wedding set on my left hand. No, it wasn't super-traditional, was a lovely hand-made piece with engraved leaves on the band and set with a white sapphire instead of a diamond, but still, the significance of those two rings worn together on that particular finger wasn't exactly something you could ignore.

Which, I assumed, was why this Brad person didn't seem interested in giving me even a second look. Fine by me—I definitely didn't want to attract the sort of attention he'd apparently been lavishing on Victoria. Yes, she also wore an engagement ring, a lovely antique piece Archie had found in a jewelry store in Gilbert, but it seemed that Brad didn't care about a diamond on your left hand if it wasn't accompanied by a matching wedding band.

Victoria spoke next, now sounding a little too relieved. "I was wondering where you'd gotten to," she said, and although her tone wasn't exactly accusatory, I could tell she hadn't been too thrilled to be left alone with predators like Brad wandering around.

"Oh, I made him keep fussing with his tie," I put in before Archie could respond. "It needed to be perfect, you know?"

This little white lie might have made Archie's eyes widen ever so slightly, but he recovered himself and said, "And I appreciated the input."

"The tie isn't going to help," Brad remarked, making absolutely no attempt to hide the disdain in his tone. "I keep telling you, Victoria—you'd do even better if you were dancing with a real professional."

Her perfectly arched brows drew together. It took a lot to rile Victoria—years of dealing with

Bridezillas had given her a thicker skin than mine—but I could tell she wanted to put the heel of her blue satin dance shoe right up Brad's behind.

But because she'd cultivated a calm I could only dream of possessing, she said smoothly, "I doubt I'd have the same bond with another partner. But thank you for the offer."

Archie's cheekbones had taken on a flush, telling me he was doing his best to contain his own temper. "And where's *your* lovely partner, Brad?"

The man gave a dismissive lift of his shoulders. "Oh, she's around somewhere. At the bar, I would guess. Sometimes I feel like I'm having to drag a mannequin around the dance floor, she's so wasted."

"That's unfortunate," Victoria said, still using the brisk but friendly tone I had no doubt she'd employed on hundreds of troublesome brides. "But if you're worried about what she's up to, then you should probably go check on her."

She slid her arm through Archie's, and, although he didn't quite smile, he did look much more relaxed than he had a few moments earlier. "And we need to get in line," he added. "You know the judges don't like us to be late."

Before Brad could say anything, the two of them stepped briskly away, leaving me to give him an awkward smile. "I need to go find my husband,"

I said. "He's waiting for me in the audience. But best of luck."

Brad sent me a smile that was almost a snarl, not much more than a baring of teeth. "I don't need luck," he shot back. "Luck is for amateurs."

After delivering that parting shot, he turned on his heel and stalked off through the crowd, most likely in search of his possibly inebriated partner.

For a second, I just stood there, one eyebrow slightly lifted. Then I let out a breath, even as I thought, *Luck might be for amateurs...but it still has a way of intervening, for good or bad.*

I'd just have to see what kind of luck awaited Brad this evening.

## 2

## Luck Be a Lady

------

EVEN IN A CROWDED AUDITORIUM, MY husband was pretty hard to miss. Yes, he'd put on the lovely charcoal gray bespoke suit I'd bought him for our wedding, and therefore was dressed similarly to a lot of the other men in attendance, but very few of them were six feet five in their sock feet and had waist-length black hair pulled back in a silver and turquoise ponytail holder.

Also, he'd been able to get a seat on the aisle, which made him even easier to spot. He slid over to the empty chair next to him so I could take the one he'd previously occupied, and sent me a questioning glance.

"Everything okay?" he asked.

Obviously, I still hadn't mastered my poker face. Maybe I shouldn't have let that nasty little backstage exchange get to me—for all I knew, Brad Masters had been playing mind games with Victoria and Archie, trying to get them off-balance before they stepped onto the dance floor—but I couldn't help feeling annoyed on my friends' behalf. Yes, the world would keep on spinning if they didn't win, and yet Victoria had told me that they were trying to go pro so Archie would be able to set up his own dance studio in Globe.

Whether there was a lot of demand for such a thing in our adopted hometown was probably a subject for debate, but I guessed he would be a good teacher, considering he already had a lot of experience in the classroom. True, he'd been teaching American history and not the foxtrot, but I had to believe some of those same skills would carry over.

As to why he hadn't told me about his ambition to open his own dance studio, I had a feeling he didn't want to say anything until it was a done deal. Also, he might have been thinking I would view his desire to move on to a different career as a sort of betrayal, considering I'd given him a job and a place to live after he emerged as a man in a world very different from the one of the early 1950s where he'd been living before a jealous witch hexed him into a cat body.

I would never view the situation that way, of course. The job at my New Age shop, Once in a

Blue Moon, had been something I'd offered him because he needed to have some visible means of support after starting his life over in twenty-first-century Globe. Because I'd gotten an extremely large inheritance a few years back from Lucien Dumond, former head of the Greater Los Angeles Necromancers Guild, I could have easily handed over a stack of cash to Archie every month and never even felt the hit.

But while he seemed to be okay with taking a not entirely necessary job, accepting money for doing nothing would never have sat right with him, and that was why he'd come to work at the store. Honestly, he'd been a bigger help than I'd first thought, mostly because he was hyper-organized thanks to all the Virgo placements in his chart, and did a much better job of keeping the books and maintaining inventory than I ever had. Also, having another person at the shop meant I had someone to keep an eye on things if I had to slip out unexpectedly to track down a clue in whatever murder investigation I was currently undertaking.

Not that murders had been exactly common in Globe lately. No, the last time any foul play had taken place in my adopted hometown had been all the way back in November, right before Thanksgiving, and ever since then, things had been pretty much smooth sailing.

And I was just fine with that. Maybe the

universe had decided to take pity on me, and I could now look forward to a happy life uninterrupted by any shady doings in our small town.

"I'm fine," I said in response to my husband's question. I supposed I could have mentioned that tense little scene between Archie and Victoria and Brad Masters, but why? It looked as though my friends were well able to handle nasty competitors, so there didn't seem to be much point in bringing it up. "It's a madhouse back there."

"I can imagine," Calvin said with a smile. He looked down at the glossy program that rested on his knees, and gave a very small shake of his head. "I'm still kind of blown away by how big this thing is."

He wasn't the only one. This was the largest competition Archie and Victoria had ever entered, and was definitely a far cry from the small, local contests held in places like nearby Payson or even in Mesa.

"Yes, Archie told me there were more than fifty couples competing tonight," I said. "I don't know how they're all going to fit on that dance floor."

Calvin craned his head slightly to look down at the wooden expanse. The audience's chairs had been placed on risers so the spectators would have a good vantage point to see all the action, but the setup still wasn't perfect. If he hadn't given me his aisle seat, I didn't know how much of the view would have been blocked by the person sitting in front of me.

And I kind of doubted the people who'd had the bad luck to sit behind him were too thrilled about how much of their own view was being obscured by his oversized frame.

"It's pretty big," he said. "But I have to assume the people running this thing know what they're doing."

Well, he had a point there. The program trumpeted that this was the Stepping Stars dancesport competition's thirtieth year, so if they didn't have it figured out by now, I doubted they ever would.

The lights in the hall dimmed, and the chattering of the crowd subsided to a dull murmur. A man wearing a tux, his gray-streaked dark hair slicked back from his high forehead, approached the podium at one end of the rectangular ballroom floor.

"Welcome to the thirtieth annual Stepping Stars dancesport event!" he called out, and everyone started clapping. Once the applause had died off, he continued. "It's been a great weekend so far, and we're just getting started. Tonight, some of the best dancers in Arizona—some of the best in the United States—will be competing on the dance floor for a chance to claim gold status...and some fabulous cash prizes as well!"

Once again, the audience erupted in applause.

Archie hadn't mentioned anything about the cash prizes to me, mostly because he was old-fashioned and thought that talking about money was crass, but I'd seen on the competition's website that the grand prize was fifty thousand dollars. No, my friends wouldn't be able to win that much, since Archie still refused to take part in the Latin dance division and it sounded as though you had to compete in the whole shebang to win the grand prize, and yet the cash winnings for the traditional side of things could be as much as twenty-five thousand, which wasn't exactly chicken feed.

First, though, he and Victoria would have to beat all those other couples, including Brad Masters and his supposedly tipsy partner.

"Now, though," the emcee went on, "it's time to meet our competitors. Music, please!"

The opening strains of "The Blue Danube" drifted from the loudspeakers, and I had to suppress a grin. I supposed the song was probably the most famous waltz out there, but I would always associate it with *Strictly Ballroom*, a movie I'd first seen when I was a kid and watched it on broadcast TV in L.A.

To be honest, the movie had been an exaggeration, of course, but its elaborate gowns and heavy makeup weren't too different from what I saw now, if not quite as stylized. The couples competing moved onto the dance floor, gliding like a bunch of colorful swans.

"Victoria's in the light blue dress," I murmured to Calvin, who nodded as our friends swung around to the side of the dance floor facing us. With her light blonde hair pulled back in a perfect twist, she appeared like a reincarnation of Grace Kelly, an impression only bolstered by the sky-colored ballgown she wore.

My husband nodded. "They look like they were born to do this," he replied, also in an undertone.

I'd thought the same thing on more than one occasion. I loved my husband more than life itself, but he'd told me when we were prepping for our wedding that he had two left feet, an observation borne out as we'd tried to get ready for our first dance.

It was fine, though. I definitely didn't harbor any ambitions to be a ballroom dancer, and Calvin had somehow managed to avoid stepping on my toes as we made our way through the opening dance at our reception, so I couldn't really ask for much more than that.

Because I knew next to nothing about ballroom dancing, I really didn't know what the judges were looking for. To my eyes, Archie and Victoria definitely seemed to be the most elegant couple out there, but that was probably my own bias speaking, since they were my friends and also so perfectly paired in a purely aesthetic sense.

Then I saw Brad Masters and his partner, separated from Victoria and Archie by two other couples, and I felt myself frown. The woman he was dancing with had bright red hair—bright enough that I guessed it wasn't completely natural, even if she might have started out as a redhead— and definitely was pretty enough, with a pert nose and a wide, friendly mouth. No, she couldn't compare to Victoria's blonde perfection, but then again, who could?

"Something wrong?" Calvin asked, again in a near-whisper, and I could only shrug.

"That guy," I replied. "The one dancing with the redhead? He was giving Victoria some trouble backstage."

At once, Calvin's brows drew together. He might have been in civvies tonight, but he still looked every inch the cop right then. "What kind of trouble?"

Maybe I shouldn't have opened my mouth. But since I'd already broached the subject, I couldn't exactly brush it aside now. "Oh, it was probably just trash talk, or him messing with them," I said. "It's only that he was trying to make it sound like Victoria would be better off dancing with him."

"She'd never do that."

"Of course not," I responded, glad that Calvin's belief in Archie's and Victoria's relationship—on and off the dance floor—was just as unwavering as mine was. "The guy's slimy. I got a really bad vibe off him. Plus, he was trying to make it sound like his partner was a drunk."

For a moment, my husband didn't respond, but only continued to watch Brad and his red-haired partner as they gracefully spun around the perimeter of the dance floor. His eyes narrowed slightly, and once again, his expression was all cop. Even though Calvin didn't discuss every detail of his job with me—mostly for confidentiality reasons —I had to believe he'd pulled over his share of drunk drivers and knew exactly which signs to look for.

"She doesn't look impaired to me," he said after a pause.

No, she didn't. Then again, for a woman in ballroom dancing, it was all about following your partner's lead. She probably could have had a drink or two before getting out there on the dance floor and known that Brad would be doing a lot of the hard work.

But no, that wasn't fair. As Ginger Rogers had once famously pointed out, she'd had to do everything Fred Astaire did, only backward and in heels. Technically, the man led, but if the woman wasn't on top of things, a routine could end in disaster pretty quickly.

Anyway, there was nothing about Brad Masters and his partner that made me think they weren't dancing at the top of their form, and once again, I had to wonder what exactly his plan had been. There was no way in the world Victoria would ever dance with anyone other than Archie, and if word got back to Brad's partner that he'd been talking smack about her, I didn't think her reaction would be exactly positive. Since I really had no idea what their relationship even was—friends? lovers? competition partners and nothing else?—I couldn't know for sure.

But that was their problem. After all, Victoria and Archie had been competing for more than six months now and doing extremely well for themselves, so I had to believe this wasn't the first time they'd dealt with jealous competitors who might have resorted to some shady tactics in order to gain an advantage. Nothing criminal, of course, but trash talk could still be problematic even if it wasn't illegal.

No, I did my best to push Brad Masters' snarky comments aside and concentrate only on the dancing, which truly was wonderful. Good thing I wasn't a judge, because I honestly didn't know how I'd ever begin to differentiate between all the couples on the floor. My friends stood out because they really did look like a couple of silver screen movie stars who'd deigned to compete with a bunch of mere mortals, but in ballroom dancing, looks definitely weren't everything.

After the waltz concluded, there was the briefest pause, and then the music started up again, this time "Begin the Beguine" as all the dancers effortlessly shifted into a foxtrot. Once again, I found myself studying their movements, trying to see if anyone made an obvious misstep, but again I couldn't really detect anything that would make one couple stand out from another. This hadn't been the case in the smaller competitions Calvin and I had attended in order to provide Archie and Victoria some much-needed moral support, where I'd noticed several couples losing the beat or—on one notable occasion—when a man actually stepped on his partner's toes.

But it seemed pretty clear to me that when people came to compete in the Stepping Stars competition, they were far past making such obvious gaffes.

After the foxtrot, the dancers moved on to a tango, and then circled back—no pun intended— to another waltz to conclude the multi-dance part of the competition. As they filed off the dance floor, the emcee came back to the stage to thank us all for attending, and to mingle with the competitors at the mixer that would take place in another hotel ballroom in twenty minutes.

Although I knew Archie hated the idea of having to rub elbows with a bunch of strangers, the mixers, while not compulsory, were just another part of the show. I'd already assured him that Calvin and I would be there to act as a buffer, so the two of us dutifully made our way to the ballroom where the social activities were being held.

This room also had a dance floor, although a much smaller one than the huge wooden expanse used for the actual competition. A three-piece jazz band played "Cheek to Cheek," although only three or four couples were out there dancing. Instead, those of us who'd come here rather than heading back to our hotel rooms or possibly leaving the resort to sample some of Scottsdale's night life had mostly headed straight for the bar.

Luckily, Calvin and I got there before the hordes really descended, and so were able to emerge with drinks in both hands, since we figured it was better to get something for Archie and Victoria when we could instead of making them stand in line all over again. And because I knew that Archie liked dry martinis and Victoria was a pinot grigio girl like me, I figured it was safe enough to place the order.

About ten minutes later, the two of them appeared, Archie out of white tie and into a tux that looked equally fabulous, if not quite so formal as his tails, and Victoria in a shimmery champagne-toned cocktail dress and high silver heels. She took the pinot grigio from me, saying, "Thank you so much. I definitely needed a drink after that multi-dance."

"You looked amazing," I said, which was only the truth.

"We did?" she responded, as if surprised by my comment.

"Of course you did," I told her, and Calvin nodded.

Archie apparently wasn't as dubious about their performance, because he said, "It went very well. Even though I hate to admit it, I think our only real competition was from Brad Masters and Joanna Greer."

Ah, so that was her name. I supposed I could have looked it up in the program, but at the time, I was too busy watching the dancers perform and didn't want to take my eyes off the dance floor.

"I think you were better than they were," Calvin commented, but Archie didn't appear convinced...probably because he knew just as well as I did that my husband wasn't exactly an expert when it came to ballroom dance.

"Let's hope the judges think so, too," Victoria said, and sipped some of her wine. "It's going to be excruciating waiting for the results. I guess I understand why they grouped them all together at the end, but still...."

I gave her a sympathetic nod. It was true—because the event stretched over four days, the awards ceremony wouldn't take place until Monday afternoon, on Memorial Day. I supposed it was a way of ensuring that people attending the competition wouldn't disappear as soon as the winners of a particular category were announced, but still, I thought it was a little rough for anyone who had to be back at work on Tuesday following the long weekend.

"It'll be fine," I said. "Besides, we're going to be playing tourist tomorrow, so that should help distract you."

She managed a wan smile, but I got the feeling that wandering around Scottsdale's shops and restaurants might not be enough to keep her mind off the results of the competition. While I didn't know much about the city, she'd lived there for more than five years before she relocated to Globe, and what would seem novel to me was probably old hat to her.

And Archie and Calvin planned to play golf, even though neither of them was huge on the game. However, I got the impression they'd rather spend their day puttering around the greens instead of getting dragged into every boutique that looked halfway interesting, so I hadn't asked too many questions.

Several people came up to Archie and Victoria then, telling them they'd really enjoyed their performance and wishing them luck. Victoria, always gracious, thanked the well-wishers for their support, and even Archie managed to smile despite looking as though he wanted to flee the room.

About forty-five minutes or so passed, during which we chatted in between sips of our drinks... and I couldn't help thinking that Archie, in his impeccable tux and with a martini in one hand, would have made a great James Bond.

Well, except for that whole not being British thing.

Then Victoria shifted her weight from one foot to the other and said, "I have got to get out of these heels. They seemed fine when I tried them on, but I guess I didn't test-drive them enough."

"Do you need to go back to the room?" Archie asked, his expression immediately one of concern.

She shook her head. "No—I have a spare pair of shoes in the trunk. Can you give me the key?"

He reached in his pocket and pulled out a plain silver fob with a single brass key hanging from it, then handed it over to her. "I can come with you," he offered.

"No, that's fine," she said quickly. "I'm just going to pop over and change my shoes, then come right back. And you haven't finished your martini yet."

That was true—Archie wasn't a huge drinker, and had the capacity to nurse a single cocktail or glass of wine for what felt like hours. Also, the hotel didn't allow people to wander the halls while carrying their drinks with them, so he would have either had to gulp it down or leave it behind while the martini was less than half drunk.

"If you're sure—" he began, and she smiled and went on her tiptoes so she could press a kiss against his cheek.

"I'm sure. I'll only be a couple of minutes."

Because she'd just finished her pinot grigio, she took the empty glass with her so she could leave it on one of the trays placed near the bar where people were supposed to deposit their used drinkware. Although I knew her feet must have been killing her, she walked briskly enough toward the exit and out into the hallway...probably because she wanted to make sure she could get those silver heels off as soon as possible.

Archie and Calvin and I made small talk in her absence, mostly because, with Archie getting interrupted every couple of minutes to acknowledge an admirer, there wasn't much point in going into anything too serious. No, we talked about the ongoing remodel at the house he and Victoria had just bought, and how she was using it as a kind of showcase of her interior decorating skills, and about the plans for their upcoming wedding, set for mid-October. Nothing that involved state secrets, or a mention of the seventy-plus years he'd spent as a smoke-gray cat roaming the streets and alleys of my adopted hometown.

Even though the ballroom around us seemed to be crowded with all the competitors and a good chunk of the spectators from the multi-dance competition, I didn't see any sign of Brad Masters, and hoped he hadn't been lying in wait in the back-stage area, hoping Victoria might return to get something out of the steamer trunk she shared with Archie.

No, that was silly. There were probably at least two hundred people crammed into the space my little group currently occupied, and I knew it was silly to think I might be able to catch a glimpse of one particular man in the crowded room.

Still, time ticked by, and I could see Archie's expression grow more and more strained. Victoria had said she would be back in five minutes, so what was taking her so long?

"Maybe I should go look for her," he murmured, and Calvin sent a worried look in my direction. Judging by his expression, I guessed he was also worried that Brad Masters might have waylaid our friend's fiancée.

"Probably a good idea," Calvin said.

I didn't argue. Yes, it was most likely nothing—the shoes she'd been looking for hadn't been in the trunk, and she'd had to go up to her hotel room after all, something like that—but better safe than sorry.

Especially since Brad Masters seemed like exactly the sort of person to wait until a woman was alone before he cornered her.

Since Calvin and I had already finished our drinks, it wasn't any hardship to set our glasses down on one of the trays by the bar, and Archie, looking resigned, placed his half-full martini next to them. As we headed out into the hallway, we noticed that the people who passed us were whispering amongst themselves while hurrying toward the exits.

Had something happened?

I hadn't heard a fire alarm go off, though, and there weren't any other competitions scheduled for the next half hour. Which meant...what?

As we approached the entrance to the backstage area, my pulse quickened. Standing guard there were four men wearing the uniform of the Scottsdale police, as well as two others in plain clothes who I guessed were probably hotel security.

Calvin approached one of the police officers. "What's going on here?"

"I'm afraid I'm not at liberty to say," the man replied. He looked like he was around Calvin's age, in his mid-thirties, but several inches shorter, with sandy hair and brown eyes.

"My fiancée is in there," Archie said, tone measured but taut at the same time, telling me he was exerting enormous effort not to push the men aside so he could go in search of his lady love.

"'Fiancée'?" the officer repeated.

"Yes," I put in. "Victoria Parrish. She competed earlier this evening."

The officer exchanged a glance with his compatriots. Looking impatient, Calvin pulled out his wallet so he could show the security detail his tribal police I.D. True, this wasn't his jurisdiction, but he'd told me on more than one occasion that cops tended to cut other cops more slack when it came to this sort of thing.

Well, unless my husband was dealing with Henry Lewis, the chief of Globe's police force. The two men had never had much use for each other, a situation that my meddling in the town's various murders hadn't exactly improved.

"We'd like to know what's going on," Calvin said, his voice measured.

The officer he was speaking to gave a very brief

nod, as if telling himself it was okay to divulge at least a little information.

"Your fiancée is all right," the man said, looking at Archie. "She's just a little shook up."

I tilted my head. "'Shook up'?" I echoed.

"Yeah," the officer replied. "She found a body in her steamer trunk."

## 3

## Bits and Pieces

VICTORIA, LOOKING PALER THAN I'D EVER seen her, sat on a folding chair while a man in a sport jacket and khakis and holding a notepad—obviously the detective assigned to the case—was asking, "Who else had a key to that trunk?"

"No one," she replied. Her gaze flicked toward Archie and Calvin and me as we approached from the side, and the relief in her expression was painfully obvious. "Tell him, Archie."

The detective glanced over at my friend. "You're the fiancé?" he asked.

"Yes," Archie said. "Archie Bradshaw. What happened?"

A pause as the detective looked over at the trunk in question—or at least, where I supposed it still sat. Someone had raised a scrim in front of it so

I couldn't really tell exactly what was going on, only that the shadows of a group of people were busy around it, gathering whatever physical evidence they could, I assumed.

Victoria pressed her lips together. A little color had begun to return to her cheeks, but she still looked utterly shocked. "I went to the trunk to get my shoes," she said. "And when I opened it, I—"

The words broke off there, as though she didn't quite have the strength to describe what she'd seen.

However, the detective stepped in, saying, "She found the body of an individual named Brad Masters."

A gasp slipped through my lips before I could hold it back. Calvin sent me a very brief glance, although his expression was impassive and I couldn't quite tell whether he was trying to offer me some reassurance or whether he was just annoyed that I'd made such a betraying noise.

"You knew Mr. Masters?" the detective asked me, his eyes narrowing slightly, and I shook my head.

"No," I replied, then quickly added, "That is, I met him very briefly right before the competition. But I definitely didn't know him."

The detective scratched something else on his notepad. "Well, that's all I need for now," he said.

His gaze flicked from Archie to Victoria as he went on, "You're staying here at the resort?"

Victoria managed a weak nod.

"Good," the detective said. "Make sure you stick around in case we have any further questions."

She pressed her lips together and inclined her head again. "Of course."

Then she got up from the folding chair where she sat, looking way too wobbly in the uncomfortable heels she still wore. At once, Archie was at her side, saying, "Let's go up to our room."

Neither Calvin nor I spoke, although I got the feeling that comment had been intended for all of us, not just Victoria. We headed out of the backstage area and over to the elevators, none of us saying anything, as if we'd all realized it was better to keep quiet until we were somewhere a little less public.

When we got to the floor where both our rooms were located, though, Archie said, "Let's get changed, and then we can all regroup and decide what to do next."

That sounded like a great idea. True, the heels I was wearing were pretty comfortable, but whatever might come next, it just seemed better to face it in something a little more practical than a cocktail dress.

So we went our separate ways, and Calvin and I

hurried into our room so we could climb out of our evening wear, and into jeans and a pretty sleeveless top for me, and cargo pants and a henley T-shirt for my husband.

Soon enough, we were over at Archie and Victoria's room and knocking at the door. When Archie answered, I saw that he'd also changed into much more casual attire—jeans and a polo shirt—although, as always, he looked like a model from a Banana Republic catalogue.

Victoria sat on a chair at the table by the window, also in jeans, but with an embroidered top in a shade of blue that echoed her eyes. A glass of water sat in front of her, although it didn't look as though she'd drunk much from it.

Calvin and I settled ourselves on the edge of the bed, since there wasn't really anywhere else to sit. "So...?" I ventured, then stopped. As much as the suspense was killing me, I had to remember that she'd just suffered a horrible shock and therefore shouldn't be pushed.

She reached for the glass of water and took a sip, then set it back down. The tremor in her hand as she did so told me she still wasn't as composed as she wanted us to believe, even if she was doing her best to hold it together.

"It was awful," she said, her voice faint. The Victoria Parrish I knew was always brisk and cheerful and composed, so seeing her as shaken as this rattled me more than I wanted to admit. "I went to the trunk and opened it, and—and—"

"And Mr. Masters was inside, stabbed in the heart," Archie finished for her. "But because the trunk wasn't big enough to accommodate him, the killer...."

He stopped as well, as if relating this particular piece of information was a little too much even for him. Next to me, Calvin stiffened, telling me he'd just put together the pieces of the terrible story.

So to speak.

"The killer cut him up?" he asked matter-of-factly, and Virginia swallowed, now looking like she wasn't sure whether she'd be able to hold down the water she'd just drunk.

I couldn't really blame her. Even allowing my brain to process the thought made the glass of pinot grigio I'd consumed at the reception gurgle uneasily in my stomach.

"Not...not all of him," she managed at last. "But his legs had been cut off and...."

"It's all right," Archie said at once. The whole time, he'd been standing next to her, holding her free hand, while she clung to him like someone who'd just escaped a shipwreck and was hanging on for dear life to the Coast Guard officer who'd rescued her. "You don't have to give us all the details."

She bit her lip, then closed her eyes and

breathed in again. "It was the most awful thing I've ever seen. I mean, I don't even watch horror movies, and to open the trunk and see that—see him—"

"I'm so sorry," I said, and wished I could provide more comfort than that. But I honestly didn't know what I could say to make the situation any better, so instead I asked, "What do you want us to do for you? Do you want to be alone with Archie? Is there anything you can think of that might help to take your mind off what happened?"

For a long moment, she didn't reply, only sat in her chair, looking thoughtful. Archie continued to hold her hand, although he shifted his weight from one foot to the other, and I got the feeling he would have preferred for her to say she wanted us to leave so he could comfort her in private.

But then she lifted her chin and said, "I think I'd like to go out somewhere. Just...someplace that isn't this hotel, isn't the place where it happened. Does that make any sense?"

"Yes, it does," Archie replied, his tone warm, reassuring. Six months ago, I would never have believed my friend the former cat could have sounded like that, but love had a way of surprising all of us.

Especially me.

"Where would you like to go?" he asked next, and now her expression grew thoughtful.

"The Brat Haus," she said after a pause. "It's this silly place with a beer garden and lots of junk food and a big patio. I want to sit outside in the sun and drink a beer...or two."

Possibly having some beer on top of the pinot grigio she'd just drunk wasn't the best idea in the world, but I knew I wasn't going to contradict her, not when she'd experienced such a horrible shock less than an hour earlier.

"Brat Haus it is," Archie replied. If he'd been hoping for a slightly more sophisticated escape, he definitely didn't show it. "How far is it from here?"

"No more than ten minutes," she said. "Parking can be tight, though, so we should all drive together."

None of us had a problem with that plan, so we decided to take my Jeep Renegade, since it had a bigger back seat than Victoria's Mercedes GLA. Just as she and I were slinging our purses over our shoulders, getting ready to head out the door, someone knocked.

Archie sent his fiancée a mystified glance. "Did you order room service?"

"Of course not," she said, sounding indignant. "Up until a minute ago, I wasn't even sure whether I'd be able to hold down any food."

Still looking puzzled, Archie went to the door and opened it. Standing outside were two uniformed officers, along with the detective who'd questioned Victoria only a half hour earlier.

"Archibald Bradshaw?" the detective said, and Archie frowned at him.

"You know that's my name."

"Yes, I do," the detective returned. "I'm here to arrest you for the murder of Brad Masters."

---

I grimly reflected that I'd spent way more of my life hanging out in police stations to post bail than I'd ever expected to. Yes, the Scottsdale P.D.'s headquarters was about as different from the tiny Globe station as the resort where we were staying was from my town's Best Western Inn, but even though the Scottsdale's police station was new and glossy and modern, that didn't mean I wanted to be spending my Friday night there.

Detective Murphy—the man who'd arrested Archie in his hotel room an hour earlier—had only told us we needed to wait to see whether the judge would allow him to post bail. That was why the three of us remained in the waiting area, not sure how long we were going to be sitting on these uncomfortable chairs, or if we would spend hours here, only to be told that the judge had denied bail and Archie would remain in jail until his trial... whenever that happened.

"I can't believe this," Victoria said for what felt like the hundredth time. Not that I could blame her. When Calvin was booked for the murder of Dillon James, a reality-show host whose show had been filming near Globe, the whole horrible situation had also possessed an air of unreality, as though some part of my brain had steadfastly refused to acknowledge the actuality of the arrest... and what it might mean for Calvin's and my future together. "Everyone knows Archie wouldn't hurt a fly!"

I wasn't sure whether that statement was precisely true, because I was pretty sure a good number of mice had met the business end of his paw during his time as a cat. But since Archie still hadn't told Victoria the truth about all those years he'd been cursed to a feline existence—a sore subject between the two of us, since I'd told him repeatedly that she was his fiancée and deserved to know—I didn't dare bring up that topic.

However, while I thought Archie might be capable of violence if pushed to the extreme...for instance, if he thought the woman he loved was in danger...there was absolutely no way in the world a man with so many Virgo placements in his chart would have resorted to a crime as messy as stabbing Brad Masters in the heart and then chopping off his arms and legs so he would fit in that steamer trunk.

Problem was, I doubted that sort of argument would sit very well with a jury.

"Archie has an alibi," Calvin said calmly. "He was either with you or with us the entire time."

This piece of supposed encouragement didn't sit as well with Victoria as my husband had probably hoped it would. She knotted her hands in her lap and replied, "Except he wasn't. He got done changing out of his competition clothes faster than I did, and he went downstairs about a half hour before me."

Odd behavior for Archie, who usually stuck pretty close to his fiancée. It wasn't that they were joined at the hip—for one thing, he spent most of his weekdays at the shop while she worked on the ongoing remodel at their house and dealt with closing out the last of her wedding clients—but at any social event, they generally didn't let each other out of their sight.

"Did he say why?" Calvin asked. His brow was ever so slightly furrowed, telling me he also thought this behavior was a little out of character.

"He said he wanted to talk to the stage manager," Victoria replied without hesitation. "Archie thought they were leaving pauses that were too big between the musical pieces, so things weren't flowing together the way we expected."

That sounded like exactly the sort of thing that

would get under Archie's skin. He always wanted everything to be just so.

And because I'd attended enough of these events by now to get a feel for how they were supposed to be run, I'd also noticed those minor gaps in the music, although I'd brushed them off as a stylistic choice and nothing more.

"Well, if Archie talked to the stage manager, then the man can corroborate his whereabouts at the time of the murder," Calvin said reasonably. "I know this must all feel awful right now, but we'll get it straightened out."

Rather than these words reassuring her, Victoria looked even more downcast. "Except Archie couldn't find the stage manager," she replied. "He said he looked all over the place, expecting to find the man somewhere backstage, but he was nowhere to be found."

Damn it. That didn't sound good. Still....

"But other people must have seen Archie," I pointed out, and she shook her head.

"Everyone had left by then to go to the reception. I mean, it had to be empty backstage, right? Otherwise, how could Brad Masters have been murdered and— you know." Victoria stopped there, an expression of something resembling grim amusement crossing her lovely, strained features. "Whoever did that to Brad, I'm pretty sure they didn't have an audience."

No, probably not. Since I wasn't really someone who watched crime dramas...despite having solved a rough half-dozen murders by this point...I honestly had no idea how long it would take to cut someone's arms and legs off, and yet I doubted it was the sort of thing you could do very quickly. Would Archie's unaccounted-for half hour even have been enough?

Obviously, Detective Murphy thought so.

And what about the mess? I didn't know a lot, but I had to believe that kind of butchery would leave behind a lot of blood.

It seemed to me that Brad Masters must have been murdered and chopped up elsewhere, and then stuffed in Archie's steamer trunk to make it look as though he was the culprit. Detective Murphy had told Victoria during their interview that it was well known among local dance circles how the two men weren't exactly besties, and there had been several witnesses to that last tense encounter between them backstage. And while the Stepping Stars judges definitely weren't talking, the consensus seemed to be that Archie and Victoria and Brad and his partner Joanna were the closest contenders when it came down to who would actually win the gold in the multi-dance competition. People had killed for a lot less than twenty-five thousand dollars, even if you didn't add the whole jealousy component to the mess.

On the surface, the whole thing probably looked like an open-and-shut case, especially when you factored in the inconvenient fact that there was only one key to the steamer trunk, and it had been in Archie's possession until he handed it over to Victoria. Since she hadn't mentioned that the trunk was unlocked when she opened it, I had to believe someone must have picked the lock.

I knew my friend was innocent...which meant the real killer must be still be out there somewhere. However, my intuition told me this had to have been a personally motivated crime, and not the work of serial killer who'd suddenly decided to start offing ballroom dance champions.

"It's all still circumstantial," Calvin said. "Being arrested is scary—believe me, I know—but I don't think they have any real evidence to prove Archie is guilty. About all we can do now is wait."

Which was what we already had been doing, for what felt like an eternity. My stomach let out a little growl, not really loud enough for anyone else to hear, reminding me that we'd been about to go out to eat before Detective Murphy appeared at the door of Archie and Victoria's room.

Well, my stomach would have to wait. If I got really desperate, I could get a granola bar or something from one of the vending machines thoughtfully placed in the police station's lobby.

"I wonder what the people running the competition are going to do now," Victoria said. I got the feeling she was talking about something inconsequential because it kept her from thinking about what she would do if the judge decided to deny bail for Archie. If that happened, he might be stuck here for months. In a small place like Gila County, where Globe was located, the wheels of justice turned a lot more quickly, just because it wasn't exactly what you could call a dense population center, but Scottsdale was located in Maricopa County, where the vast majority of Arizona's inhabitants lived. I didn't want to contemplate how impacted the local docket must be.

"Do you think they'll cancel the rest of the competition?" Calvin asked. I wasn't sure whether he was genuinely curious, or whether he'd also realized it was best to keep Victoria distracted while we sat here and waited to learn Archie's fate.

She gave a small shrug. "I don't know," she replied. Sitting there on the hard plastic chair, she looked thinner and frailer than she really was, probably because of the dejected slump of her shoulders. "I'm pretty sure nothing like this has ever happened before. Sure, sometimes people have to drop out of competitions because of health issues or whatever, but that's not the same thing as having someone murdered backstage."

No, it definitely wasn't. The homicide team had still been working on the scene when we left, so even if the organizers of the event decided to resume the competition tomorrow, definitely nothing else was going to happen tonight.

"Well, there's one way to find out," I said, and dug my phone out of my purse. I still had the information for the Stepping Stars event on the iPhone's Safari browser, so I refreshed the web page to see if they'd made any kind of announcement. It was entirely possible they were holding off until they got more information from the police, but....

No, there it was.

*Due to unforeseen and tragic circumstances, the remainder of this year's Stepping Stars awards are being postponed. Check back later for more information.*

That was all, but at least it told me the organizers weren't going to abandon the event entirely. I had to imagine the logistics of moving such a large-scale function to a different weekend were going to take some time, so at this point, all anyone could do was wait to see what happened.

Not that I was overly concerned about the ballroom dance competition itself. No, Archie's fate was much more important.

All the same, I relayed what I'd found to Calvin and Victoria. He only nodded, as if he didn't find this latest development too surprising, but Victoria frowned.

"I was sure they'd just cancel it," she murmured.

"I guess they decided that wouldn't be fair to all the other dancers," I said. "But it sounds like it's pretty up in the air for now."

We all fell silent then, each of us occupied with our own thoughts. The Goddess only knew what must be going through Victoria's head right then, although I told myself this would all get straightened out eventually, even if I had to track down the killer myself.

That thought made a little chill run down my spine. It was one thing to roam around in Globe and do my amateur Nancy Drew act there—even if my "meddling" was enough to raise Henry Lewis's blood pressure by several points—and something else entirely to start poking around in Scottsdale, where I had to believe their large and very efficient-seeming police force might have an issue with someone like me sticking her nose in where it didn't belong.

A deputy approached us, the same fresh-faced woman who'd guided us to the waiting area a few hours earlier. "Detective Murphy would like to speak to you," she said.

At once, we got up from our chairs. "All of us?" Victoria asked.

"Yes," the deputy said. "This way."

Knowing I probably wore the same mystified

expression on my face that Victoria did, I tagged along as the deputy led us out of the waiting area and down a long corridor lined with offices. Near the end of the hall, she stopped and knocked on the door in front of us.

"Detective Murphy?"

"Come in."

The deputy opened the door, but stood out of the way so the three of us could enter. Although the detective's office was larger and definitely had newer carpet on the floor, it still reminded me of Henry Lewis's domain at the Globe police station, mostly because the desk here was also covered in stacks of file folders and had the same air of organized chaos.

Detective Murphy sat behind that desk, his expression sour. He didn't look particularly pleased to see any of us, and I wondered why he'd asked for this audience.

"The judge granted bail," he said, which I thought might have accounted for the annoyed look on his face. In the next second, though, I thought I caught a hint of glee in his voice as he added, "One million dollars."

Clearly, he harbored the opinion that there was no way in the world Victoria—or any of the rest of us—could come up with even the ten percent of that sum required to get a bail bond outfit to agree to get Archie sprung from jail.

On her own, I wasn't sure whether Victoria could. She'd made a decent amount off the sale of her condo, true, but she'd plowed pretty much all of that money right back into the house she'd bought with Archie, and I knew she was only working with a few wedding clients at the moment, trying to gracefully phase out that part of her professional life so she could move into interior decorating full time.

But what Detective Murphy didn't know was that I had many times that amount stashed in various bank accounts, all thanks to the money Lucien Dumond had left me two years earlier. I'd made a lot of charitable donations and hadn't exactly been watching my spending, and yet those accounts only seemed to grow with each passing year.

"No problem," I said serenely, and the detective blinked. "Will the bailiff accept a personal check, or will I need to wait until tomorrow morning so I can get a cashier's check from my bank?"

That question earned me another blink. Clearly, he hadn't expected any of us to be quite so nonchalant about the situation. However, his tone was brisk enough as he said, "I'd suggest seeing a bail bondsman...unless you're okay with having your friend spend the night in jail."

We most definitely were not, and I told him as

much. Having delivered his news, he seemed content to inform us about the most reliable bail bondsmen in the area, and then usher us out of his office and back to the lobby.

Why he hadn't asked his deputy to provide this information instead, I didn't know, although I got the impression he was hoping we wouldn't be able to afford Archie's bail and wanted to see our disappointment for himself. Definitely a jerk maneuver, but it seemed obvious to me that he thought Archie was guilty and wasn't too happy about the prospect of him being released to possibly kill again.

Well, that wasn't going to happen. Or at least, I didn't know for sure whether this was a one-off crime or whether the killer was about to leave a trail of tuxedo-clad bodies behind him, but I did know that it wouldn't be Archie committing those murders.

To my relief, the bail bondsman took a personal check, and after another hour or so of tedious paperwork and so on, Archie emerged from where they'd been keeping him in a holding cell, looking slightly weary but otherwise unscathed. To be honest, if I hadn't known he'd spent the last few hours behind bars, I would have thought he'd passed a quiet evening watching TV and was now ready to call it a night.

Victoria hurried over and threw her arms

around him, and he held on to her for a long moment, his face buried in her hair. Then he let go of her and looked over at Calvin and me, his expression almost embarrassed.

An incongruous smile touched his lips. "Anyone still hungry?"

## 4

## All in the Cards

ARCHIE STEADFASTLY REFUSED TO TALK about his ordeal in the Scottsdale jail, and instead was interested to hear about how the competition had been postponed but not canceled.

"So...technically, we could still compete," he said after washing down a bite of brat, and Victoria looked at him as though he'd lost his mind.

"We are *not* competing," she replied. "We're going to lie low and wait to see what the police investigation turns up."

He lifted an eyebrow. To all our infinite relief, the Brat House stayed open until 1 a.m. on Friday and Saturday nights, and that meant we'd been able to go straight there from the police station and get some much-needed food in our stomachs. The place was crowded even at that hour, probably because of the long holiday weekend, but we were still able to snag a long table off to one side. And since it was Scottsdale in late May, even though it was past midnight, the temperature hovered around eighty degrees and we were able to sit outside in our shirtsleeves and feel extremely comfortable.

Or at least as comfortable as we could be, knowing that a cloud of suspicion hovered over Archie's head. The arraignment had been set for the following Wednesday, and although Calvin had opined that he didn't think the judge would revoke bail, we still didn't know for sure. So much could happen between now and then, the happiest outcome being that the Scottsdale P.D.'s homicide unit would find the real killer during that time.

Unfortunately, I didn't think it would be turn out to be that easy.

"Innocent until proven guilty, my dear," Archie said, and reached for the pitcher of beer that sat in the middle of the table so he could refill his glass. Most of the time, my friend wasn't much of a beer guy, but he probably wasn't too worried about being discriminating at the moment.

"It still wouldn't look good," Victoria said. "I mean, the police already think you did it. If you go and compete, it's going to look like you're taking advantage of Brad Masters' death."

That particular angle obviously hadn't occurred to Archie, because his brow furrowed and he was silent for a moment. "Possibly," he allowed, although it didn't seem as if he was willing to go any further than that.

"There'll be other competitions," she said, and laid her hand on his where it sat on the tabletop. "I really think it's better to let it go."

He released a breath but didn't say anything, seeming to signal he would consider her words... even if he didn't like them very much.

And that, for the moment at least, seemed to be that.

---

Although none of us really wanted to stay at the hotel, we were all forced to admit it probably wouldn't be a good idea to drive back to Globe at one in the morning, especially after sharing a pitcher of beer. Instead, we went to our separate rooms, promising one another that we'd meet for breakfast at ten at a restaurant Victoria knew, and then drive home after that.

Once I'd closed the hotel room door behind me, I allowed myself a big sigh. "Not exactly the way we'd pictured this evening ending," I remarked, and Calvin gave an understanding nod.

"No," he said. "But at least Archie isn't stuck in jail, and tomorrow we can go home and try to regroup."

True. All the same, I wished I could just wiggle my nose and send us all straight back to Globe so we could sleep in our own beds.

Unfortunately, I wasn't that kind of witch. Yes, I had a little garnet pendulum tucked into my purse, just in case I needed to perform a bit of divination on the go, but something told me now wasn't the time to be asking it any questions. My instincts seemed to indicate it would be better to go home so I could work in the lovely, peaceful bedroom I'd turned into my office, surrounded by the things I loved most. The energy there would be much more helpful in guiding me to discover the identity of the real killer.

Archie hadn't come out and asked me to help, and yet I knew I would do this for him, just like I'd worked to exonerate my friend Josie back in November, or Calvin more than a year ago, when Henry Lewis had been convinced that my husband had killed Dillon James in a fit of jealous rage. But whatever odd gift helped me navigate those messages from the universe wouldn't be working in top form here, in a hotel surrounded by the jangly energy of hundreds of other people, so I realized I had to let it go.

That energy felt even janglier the next morning when the four of us emerged from the hotel lobby...only to be besieged by a mob of reporters who descended as soon as we walked out into the merciless morning sunlight.

"Mr. Bradshaw, can you tell us anything about what happened on Friday night?"

"Mr. Bradshaw, care to comment on your relationship with the victim?"

"Mr. Bradshaw, are you going to come back and compete?"

Thank the Goddess that we had Calvin with us. He might not have been a professional bodyguard, but he still did an excellent job of interposing his nearly six and a half feet between Archie and the gang of reporters, somehow managing to keep them at bay while guiding our little group away from the hotel and into our vehicles. Because we'd already planned to caravan home, I'd parked my Renegade next to Victoria's lipstick-red Mercedes SUV, so it wasn't too hard for us to slip inside the vehicles and shut out the microphone mob.

Going out to eat suddenly didn't sound like such a good idea. Since Calvin was driving, I got out my phone and texted Archie.

> Can you wait until we get to
> Globe to eat? We can go straight
> to The Flatiron.

> Probably a good idea.

Yes, that meant it would be close to noon by the time we sat down to eat, but the restaurant served breakfast until one, and in our hometown, we had a much better chance of breaking our fast without having to worry about a bunch of reporters mobbing the place.

Even as it was, several of their news vans followed us to the freeway, then gave up the chase after we pulled onto the eastbound on-ramp. I didn't know why they'd decided against trailing us all the way back to Globe, but maybe they'd decided the story wasn't worth a round trip of almost three hours, especially when they didn't have much to go on except the barest facts of Brad Masters' death and the way Archie had been arrested for his murder only an hour or so later.

Despite the lack of pursuit, I didn't find myself relaxing until we'd passed Queen Creek and were truly out of the Phoenix sprawl. Although Calvin had kept his eyes on the road the whole time, he still must have sensed the way I let myself rest against the back of the seat, asking, "Doing okay over there?"

"Better now that we're closer to home," I replied, and he nodded.

"I know what you mean. I'm not exactly a big-city guy myself."

No, he wasn't. He'd left Globe for a few years to get his degree in criminal justice at ASU in

Phoenix, but he'd come straight back as soon as his studies were completed. And even though I'd grown up in the San Fernando Valley and had spent most of my adult life in Los Angeles proper, I didn't miss it a bit. Something about the wild landscapes of Arizona, the open spaces and the blue, blue skies, soothed my soul in a way city sprawl never could.

We were silent for a couple of minutes. Then I said, "Do you think they really have a case against Archie?"

Calvin released a breath. Still with his eyes on the road, he replied, "Well, they had enough of a case that the Scottsdale P.D. felt pretty safe arresting him. It's encouraging that the judge allowed bail, though."

"A million dollars' worth," I said gloomily. No, I wasn't worried about the hundred grand I'd had to plunk down to get Archie out of jail, but the mere fact that the bail amount had been set so high told me the judge was taking the case very seriously.

"Better than no bail at all," Calvin told me, and I didn't bother to argue when I knew he was right. Maybe things weren't looking so great right now, but at least Archie had been released, albeit with the restriction that he couldn't leave the state.

No huge hardship, since my friend hadn't once set foot outside Arizona after resuming his human form. Maybe that was because he'd been so busy the whole time, he hadn't felt any need to travel, or possibly it was more that he didn't want to stress-test the false documents, including a driver's license and Social Security card, that Calvin had procured for him. I still wasn't exactly sure how my husband had pulled that off, and the few times I'd tried to ask a few questions about the provenance of those faux I.D.s, he'd told me the less I knew, the better, so I'd let it go.

All the same, I allowed myself to be just the tiniest bit reassured that those documents hadn't raised any eyebrows with the Scottsdale P.D. If there had been even the slightest whiff of impropriety, I had a feeling the judge would never have granted Archie bail.

Just as we were entering Globe's city limits—and right after I got a cell signal again, since there was a pretty big dead spot in the mountainous stretch of highway between my adopted hometown and Miami, the next settlement over—my phone pinged.

Archie.

> We've decided to go straight home. Victoria thinks it might be better for us to keep a low profile for a while.

I allowed myself a pang of disappointment, even as I realized their decision was probably for the best. Although Archie had become much more of a known quality around town over the course of the past twelve months, he still was viewed as something of an outsider, and that meant some people in the town probably wouldn't be as quick to jump to his defense as they might have for someone they'd known all their lives.

> Okay. How about you come over for a barbecue tonight?

That seemed like a safe enough suggestion. After all, Calvin's and my home was located a few miles outside Globe, down a private road with no other houses on it. If we weren't safe from prying eyes there, we wouldn't be safe anywhere. And because I'd already closed down my shop for the weekend so Archie and I could attend the competition, it wasn't as if I needed to worry about rushing back to Once in a Blue Moon and trying to salvage some sales on what would normally have been a fairly busy shopping day.

> That sounds good. Victoria wants to know if we should bring anything.

> Just some wine.

I left it at that, mostly because I knew that Victoria, although possessed of many sterling qualities, wasn't what you could call much of a cook. From what I could tell, Archie did most of the food prep in their household, and I certainly wasn't going to ask him to whip up some potato salad or whatever, not with everything he currently had weighing on his mind.

> We can do that. What time?

> Six-thirty?

> We'll see you then.

The convo ended there, but that was fine. I could trust the couple to bring something fun to drink, and they could look forward to a relaxing evening where they wouldn't be bothered by anyone.

As for me, I knew we had a luscious tri-tip in the fridge that I'd picked up at the store the day before we left for Scottsdale, figuring Calvin and I could have a barbecue after we got back. Luckily, it was big enough to feed all four of us, and I'd whip up cowboy beans and salad and green chile corn-bread, and then a batch of the butterscotch choco-late chip cookies Archie loved so much. Whether or not a spread like that would be enough to distract him from the legal troubles that loomed over him like a thundercloud from a particularly fierce monsoon storm, I didn't know, but I figured it couldn't hurt to try.

I related these plans to Calvin, and he nodded, looking approving. "You still want to go to The Flatiron, or would you rather go straight home, too?"

"Might as well go home," I said, trying not to sound too resigned. I'd been looking forward to some of the Flatiron's marvelous *huevos rancheros*, but I could live without them and instead put together a couple of omelets at the house. Maybe Calvin and I wouldn't attract as much attention without having Archie and Victoria with us, and yet it just seemed smarter to also maintain a low profile for a while.

"Got it," Calvin said, and didn't comment further. It could have been because he also understood the wisdom of lying low for a bit...or it could simply have been that he knew he'd get just as good a meal at home as he would at a restaurant.

And I, kitchen witch that I was, didn't mind a bit.

We had to make a brief stop at our friends Chuck and Hazel's ranch to pick up our dog Sadie, who they'd been watching for the weekend. Clearly, they hadn't been paying much attention to the news, because neither of them asked anything about Archie, although Hazel expressed surprise about us coming back so early, since the original plan was to retrieve Sadie late on Monday.

"I'll tell you about it later," I promised Hazel, and although her well-arched brows tilted slightly in curiosity, she must have seen something in my expression that told her this wasn't the time for questions. Instead, she said that was fine, and then waved goodbye as Calvin and I bumped our way down the dirt road that led back to the highway. The whole time Sadie was doing her best to lick the makeup off my face, her tail wagging at lightspeed as she demonstrated her happiness at seeing her people again.

There hadn't been any sign of Hazel's husband Chuck when we stopped at the house, but I didn't find that too surprising. It was a bright, sunny day, and he was probably out riding his three hundred or so acres, checking on the cattle and horses—and goats, too, since they were a new addition to the ranch, something Hazel had suggested.

Anyway, the rest of our drive back to the house was pretty uneventful, except for the part where Sadie kept trying to climb into Calvin's lap and he kept gently shooing her back.

"Not while he's driving, baby," I told her for the umpteenth time, and eventually she settled for standing on my legs so she could look out the window as we drove.

There wasn't anything to see that she hadn't seen a hundred times before, but I'd learned long ago that such niceties didn't matter to a dog. No, she was panting and smiling like we'd taken her on a huge adventure, a smile that only broadened after we went into the house and I got out the fixings for green chile cheddar omelets. We didn't feed her eggs because we'd learned the hard way early on that her tummy couldn't handle them, but she was a fiend for cheese.

It all felt so comfortably domestic, with Calvin taking our luggage into the main bedroom while I cracked eggs and fed little bits of shredded cheddar to the dog. The day was warm, although here in the mountains to the east of Phoenix, temperatures were still pleasant enough that I didn't see the need to turn on the A/C.

No, instead I opened all the nearby windows so a warm, friendly breeze could blow through the space, bringing with it the scent of sun-dried grass and the brisk fragrance of juniper, smells that blended nicely with the aroma of the omelets as they cooked on the stovetop. Calvin came back into the kitchen and bent down so he could kiss me on the cheek.

"It's good to be home," he said.

"It is," I agreed, and found myself wishing that

none of us had gone to that wretched competition in Scottsdale. If Archie and Victoria had decided to sit it out, then he wouldn't be staring down the barrel of a murder charge.

*Enough of that,* I scolded myself. None of this was Archie's fault. He and Victoria had been pursuing their dream, and had run into some singularly bad luck.

But bad luck could be changed, and I knew that was what we all needed to focus on. I could only hope we'd be able to come up with a workable plan to clear his name.

In the meantime, though, Calvin and I had a pleasant breakfast despite everything, and afterward, while he cleaned up—our arrangement was that whoever cooked didn't have to do dish duty— I headed toward my office. Now that I was home, and about as rested and relaxed as I was going to be, I knew I needed to do some investigating, hedgewitch style.

Everything on my altar was where I'd left it, of course, the crystals glimmering in the sunlight that slipped through the east-facing window, the faint scent of incense still hanging in the air, even though it had been several days since I burned any.

But I got out a stick of my favorite white cedar incense and lit it with the Aim-N-Flame I kept in my desk drawer, and waited a moment until a thin trail of the white, aromatic smoke began to drift upward from the end of the stick. With the room now ready for me to reach out to the universe and ask for answers, I went to the bookcase and got down my favorite Everyday Witch Tarot deck, along with the fluorite pendulum I planned to use for backup in case the cards weren't ready to provide me with any illumination today.

Sadie had followed me into the room—after waiting to see whether Calvin had any morsels to feed her before he put the plates in the dishwasher, of course—and went and settled herself into the little brown velvet bed I had placed under the window. Her presence wasn't a disruption, though, but rather, yet another comforting note in the space, reassuring me that all was as it should be.

Well, almost. I somehow doubted Archie and Victoria currently shared that same uplifting view of the world.

*I'll fix it,* I thought, and sent that intention and those words of reassurance winging out into the universe, knowing that things usually worked out the way they were supposed to.

However, that didn't mean I couldn't give the universe a helping hand.

I picked up the Tarot cards and shuffled them and shuffled them, waiting for the little tingle or twinge or whatever you wanted to call it that was my signal from the deck, indicating it was ready to impart its wisdom. This process took longer than usual, but I wouldn't allow myself to get impatient. No, I had to wait and let myself be open to whatever the Tarot had to say.

Finally, though, it seemed as if they were ready, because a tiny little twinge in the palm of my right hand told me the cards didn't want to be shuffled any longer. The whole time, I'd held a single question in my head.

*Who really killed Brad Masters?*

It wasn't that I expected the cards to spell out someone's name. If it were that easy, I would have used my pendulum and a divining board inscribed with the letters of the alphabet. But I tended to vibe better with the Tarot, and knew the clues the cards provided were often extremely helpful...as long as I was up to the task of correctly interpreting what they had to say.

The first card I laid down on my altar was the Five of Wands. "Five" cards often indicated conflict, just because the numerology of five was connected to war, people being at odds. In this case, with the Five of Wands appearing first in the reading, I knew it must be connected to competition of some sort.

Not exactly a stretch, considering that Brad had been killed at the state's biggest ballroom dance tournament. But was his murder connected to the contest itself, or had it merely provided a convenient venue for someone to settle a score?

Hard to say without a lot more details.

The next card I laid down was the Queen of Swords, reversed. When I was doing a Tarot reading as an affirmation for myself or for a friend, I didn't really do reversals, but in this case, I knew I couldn't ignore the positioning of the card. In general, the Queen of Swords represented a wise, mature woman, one in control of herself and her world. However, when reversed, she could also represent jealousy, scheming.

Had Brad Masters been killed by a woman?

On the surface, such a prospect didn't seem very likely. Not because I couldn't believe a woman was capable of murder—Miriam Jacobsen's plotting to get her hands on the Victorian mansion my parents had bought was proof enough of that unfortunate truth—but more because of the manner in which Brad had been killed. Stabbing him in the heart wouldn't have been horribly difficult, but then hacking off his arms and legs and stuffing him in that trunk?

I didn't know. Maybe a woman who competed in Olympic deadlifting or something requiring that kind of sheer muscle power would be able to manage such a feat, but I knew I sure hadn't seen anyone like that at the Stepping Stars competition. Generalizations could be troubling, and yet, the female ballroom dancers I'd encountered tended to be slender, probably so their partners could dip them and lift them as the choreography required.

Still, the murderer didn't necessarily have to be someone involved in ballroom dance. Maybe it had been an outside grudge of some sort.

But then why would the first card I turned up be the Five of Wands, indicating some kind of competition was involved?

So far, this wasn't making a lot of sense.

However, I still had the third card to pull. Something told me not to take it from the top of the deck, the way I had with the other two, but to draw it from the center. I fished it out and laid it down next to the Queen of Swords, her gaze imperious even with her image upside down.

The Magician.

In general, the Magician card was a positive one, indicating personal power and strength, or possibly hinting at a strong, beneficent ally. But in this context, I honestly couldn't see what he had to do with the other cards I laid down on my altar.

What could be positive about a man being brutally murdered?

I didn't have a clue.

For a long moment, I stood there, staring down at the cards, willing them to give me some sort of sign as to how they could all be connected. However, the images on them didn't provide any further enlightenment. In fact, I thought I saw just the slightest disdain on the face of the Queen of Swords, as though she was thinking I must be a real dullard if I couldn't put the pieces together.

I sighed, then shuffled the cards back into the deck. Right then, I had no idea what they were trying to tell me, but long experience had taught me that I couldn't force them to reveal their secrets. No, all I could do was let the images of those cards dance around in my brain, and maybe eventually I'd be able to figure it all out.

In the meantime, though, I had some cowboy beans to make.

## 5

## Undercover Angel

ALTHOUGH I THOUGHT ABOUT DISCUSSING my latest card pull with Calvin, I decided I should leave it aside, at least for the moment. He'd learned a little about the Tarot after hearing me talk about it for the past couple of years, but he wasn't an expert by any means, and since I myself didn't have a clue as to what that particular sequence of cards was supposed to mean, I doubted he'd have any particular insights to offer.

However, he had made himself useful by reaching out to the San Ramon Apaches' tribal attorney, Alec Scurlock, who didn't seem to have a problem with talking business on a holiday weekend. No, he'd told Calvin that he had several people in mind who would do well by Archie, and provided their contact information so Calvin could get in touch with them on Tuesday once we were safely past Memorial Day.

I had to hope Archie would appreciate the help. He hadn't mentioned anything about an attorney, but securing one was the obvious next step. And because this was the first time my friend had required legal help after emerging into this new life, it only made sense that Calvin, who was the one with the most contacts in that area, would be the one to begin the search.

True, I was pretty sure my friend Josie, the town's mayor and its foremost real estate agent, could have also supplied similar information, but I was feeling reticent about contacting her. Maybe she'd already heard about Archie's legal troubles and maybe she hadn't, but I didn't see the need to stir the pot. Also, the two of them were polite around each other but definitely weren't what you could call friendly—no huge surprise when dealing with two such strong personalities. Josie would never tell me when her birthday was, partly because she said she didn't want to make a big deal of it at her age...which I thought was a little silly, since she could only be in her middle fifties at the very most...and partly because I could tell she didn't want me to do her chart and perform the astrological equivalent of a psychological analysis on her.

But I'd been studying astrology long enough to guess that she was probably either a Capricorn...

smart, stubborn, concerned about material success...or possibly an Aries, who tended to be fiery, take-charge types. Either way, I could see how both signs might clash with a practical, meticulous Virgo like Archie, since I couldn't stop thinking about my two friends as the irresistible force meeting the immovable object.

However, I had to hope that, since I hadn't heard from Josie and she was the type to be on the phone...or in my shop, which wouldn't work this weekend because the store was closed...just as soon as a piece of juicy gossip dropped in her lap, so far she remained blissfully ignorant of the way my supposed "cousin" had just been charged with first-degree murder. And because I wanted the situation to stay quiet for as long as possible, that meant not asking her if she had any legal references she might want to pass along.

Victoria and Archie showed up promptly at six-thirty, just as I'd expected them to. Being late was anathema to my former-cat friend, and Victoria had way too much experience planning weddings and other large-scale events to ever be so rude.

She handed me a tote bag that held a bottle of cabernet and a bottle of zinfandel, saying, "We couldn't really decide on which one to bring. Also...."

The words trailed off, but I knew exactly what

she was thinking. "Also, this is the kind of situation where one bottle just won't be enough," I remarked.

She grinned, and even Archie, who still looked strained and worried, smiled a little at my comment. "You really need to include 'mind reader' on your resume, Selena," he told me.

I shook my head, even as I responded, "No, I'm not that kind of psychic. But I think we all know each other well enough by now that figuring out what we're going to think in a certain situation isn't that hard."

Archie conceded the point by inclining his head the littlest bit, and then we all pressed on into the house, where the beans had been cooking on high in the crockpot all afternoon, and where the tri-tip—now covered in Calvin's signature spice rub—sat on the kitchen island, coming up to room temperature in preparation for grilling.

"Some white sangria?" he asked, since he'd been in the middle of setting out the meat on its platter when our guests arrived. "Selena and I whipped up a batch this afternoon."

On other occasions, Archie might have declined, thinking he shouldn't drink more than the two bottles we were all going to share. However, after spending a large chunk of his Friday night in a holding cell, he apparently thought it was a good idea to smooth down the rough edges a bit, because he said, "That would be wonderful. Thank you."

We spent a few minutes pouring glasses for everyone, and then afterward, our little group moved out onto the patio. Calvin and I had already decided we should eat outside at the table there since it was a beautiful day and, because the house was located in such an isolated spot, it wasn't as though we'd have to worry about anyone over-hearing us.

For a little while, we just sipped sangria and chatted about the weather, although Calvin had to excuse himself after a moment or two so he could go inside and grab the platter with the tri-tip. I could tell that Archie and Victoria wanted to avoid discussing what had happened the night before, and I didn't press them. Sooner or later, that fraught topic would have to come up.

Which it did, after Calvin was done with the tri-tip and I'd brought out all the side dishes. Sadie prowled her way around the table, obviously trying to decide who she should importune for those all-important scraps of grilled meat.

As usual, she went after Archie first, because she somehow knew he was a complete pushover when it came to feeding her table scraps. I knew he and Victoria had been talking about getting a dog, but with their house only halfway remodeled, they seemed to think it best to wait a while longer. I'd asked him once if he'd ever thought about having a cat for a pet, and the look of horror he'd sent me was so genuine, I knew I'd never bring up the topic again.

Clearly, he hadn't gotten over spending seven decades in a feline body.

But after Archie had fed Sadie a few small bits of tri-tip, and after everyone's plates and glasses had been filled, Calvin said, "I've got some attorney references for you, if you need them."

Archie had been in the middle of swallowing a mouthful of cowboy beans, so he didn't answer right away. When he spoke, however, he sounded both dejected and resigned.

"I suppose that is the next step."

"It is," Victoria said, and drank some of her zinfandel. We'd decided to open that bottle first, although, since we were already halfway through it, I had no doubt the cab would soon follow. "I have an attorney on retainer, but he only handles contracts and that sort of thing." She paused there, her expression curious. "How were you able to get hold of anyone over a holiday weekend?"

"Oh, the San Ramon Apache have a tribal lawyer," Calvin said. "He's pretty much on call twenty-four/seven, but I also figured if he was busy, I'd just leave him a voicemail and he'd get back to me. Anyway, he had some good recommendations, so I'll give those to you before you leave tonight."

Archie absorbed this, expression so neutral that I could tell he secretly hated the idea of having to reach out to an attorney at all when everyone knew he was innocent.

Or at least, everyone sitting at this table knew he hadn't committed any crimes. I was sure Detective Murphy—and the organizers of the Stepping Stars dancesport competition—probably had a very different view of the situation.

"We really appreciate that," Victoria said, obviously wanting to make sure Calvin and I both knew they were grateful, even if Archie wasn't about to come out and say so.

"Yes," he said, his tone almost absent. He set down his fork and reached for his wine glass, then added, "But obviously, the best way to make all this go away would be to discover the identity of the real killer."

"True," I allowed, not daring to look over at Calvin. Although by this point he was pretty much resigned to the way I involved myself in any murders that occurred in Globe...or, in this case, involved one of my friends...I knew he still wasn't all that thrilled about it. "I did a card spread about it this afternoon, but it didn't tell me much."

Pretty much any other group of people might have shown at least a hint of skepticism at a comment like that, but Calvin and my friends knew my way of communicating with the universe was real and actually yielded results, if not always in the manner or on the timetable I would have preferred.

Frowning slightly, Archie asked, "What did it say?"

I also reached for my wine glass, and allowed myself a sip of zinfandel before replying, "Not a lot that made sense. Something about competition, but that kind of goes without saying. And there seems to be a woman involved somehow, although I get the feeling she's not the actual murderer."

"Like maybe Brad's partner Joanna?" Victoria said. She wore a hopeful light in her eyes that told me she thought that little snippet was a lot more important than I'd let on.

I responded, "I don't know. I pulled the card for the Queen of Swords, and that usually indicates someone older and wiser."

"The cards aren't strictly representational, though, right?" Calvin put in. He'd just helped himself to another piece of tri-tip, which meant Sadie was now dancing attendance on him, but he seemed to be doing his best to ignore her—not to be mean, but because she'd already gotten plenty of tidbits from the rest of us.

"Not always," I said. "Usually, mental state is more important than appearance. Still, I don't know why Brad's partner would want to kill him."

"Other than because he was a prize jackass?"

Victoria asked with a grin, and I couldn't help smiling back at her.

After all, she was totally correct in that assessment.

"Yep, besides that," I replied. "But you'd know better than I. Are there any other men competing in the contests here in Arizona who would have a better chance of winning than Brad Masters?"

For a moment, both Archie and Victoria were silent, clearly pondering my question. Then Archie shook his head.

"Other than me, not really," he said.

The response wasn't bravado—Archie really was that good, thanks to getting lots of early training back before he'd been a cat, not to mention spending almost an entire year practicing with Victoria.

No, he'd answered me in a matter-of-fact way, just to let me know that, if I was considering possible rivals as candidates for the murder suspect, there really weren't many of them out there.

Although I'd circled back to square one during a murder case many times before this, that didn't mean I had to like this sensation of being completely flummoxed. Problem was, I simply didn't have enough information to work with. I wasn't part of the ballroom dance scene, other than attending some local competitions. The other dancers were mostly names in a program to me, not individuals whose hopes and dreams—and motives —I already kind of knew.

I said as much, and Archie's eyes narrowed, telling me he didn't like having to accept that particular bitter truth. As he reached for his glass of wine, though, Victoria's expression suddenly brightened.

"I've got it!" she exclaimed.

"Got what?" I asked, hoping I didn't sound too suspicious. No, Victoria wasn't the type to cook up crazy schemes like Josie had on several notable occasions, but since she was currently fighting to keep the man she loved out of prison, I had to believe she was plotting something.

"On the way over here, I got a group text from the organizers of the competition," she said. "They've already rescheduled the competition for June tenth and eleventh. I'm not sure how they managed to get it going again so quickly, since it'll be in the same venue. I guess the resort didn't have anything big going on that weekend."

A weekend that followed Calvin's and my first wedding anniversary, which fell on June fourth. Luckily, we hadn't made plans to go out of town, instead thinking that maybe we'd just drive into Gilbert for the day and have a nice dinner there.

"And?" I returned. After all, just that morning Victoria had emphatically told Archie they weren't going to return to the competition even if it was rescheduled. But now she was actually planning to attend?

As it turned out, that wasn't quite what she had in mind.

"Like you said," she explained, "you don't know enough about the players involved to have a good frame of reference. But even though they've shrunk the remainder of the competition to two days, they're still going to be having contests for both amateurs and pros. You can go undercover at the competition and see what you dig up."

Victoria's proposition was so off the wall that for a second or two, I could only stare back at her in astonishment. Then I found my voice and replied, my tone flat, "I'm not a ballroom dancer."

"You don't have to be," Victoria said, obviously undeterred by my overwhelming lack of enthusiasm for her plan. "You'll be dancing in the novice category."

Calvin, not looking too thrilled himself, put in, "Even dancing with other beginners, I don't think the two of us would do too well."

"Oh, you wouldn't be dancing with Selena," Victoria responded at once. A small smile played around her mouth before she added, "No offense, Calvin, but I saw the two of you dance at your reception."

Rather than being offended by her remark, my husband only leaned back in his chair, glass of zinfandel in one hand. "Then who would she be dancing with?"

"Good question," Victoria said. She glanced over at Archie and asked, "Who do we know who could partner with Selena?"

Archie considered this query for a moment, then replied, "I think Eddie Bixby is available. He and his partner were supposed to dance at the Stepping Stars competition, but she sprained her ankle just the day before, so they had to drop out. And they're technically still in the novice category, although they'd hoped to move up this time. So, that means he would be a perfect partner for Selena."

Personally, I thought the situation was far from perfect. I didn't want to dance in the competition at all, let alone with a perfect stranger. "Do you know Eddie well?" I asked.

Victoria nodded. "Well enough," she said. "I mean, it's not like we all went out on double dates together or anything, but he and his partner Liza have been together since Archie and I started doing the ballroom dance circuit. He seems like a decent person—and I know he'd love to still get a chance to compete in the Stepping Stars competition."

"With someone who doesn't know a rumba from a cha-cha," I said dourly, and my friend just smiled.

"Oh, you'll pick it up quickly enough," she

assured me. "Besides, Eddie wasn't doing the Latin portion of the competition, either. You just need to worry about the waltz and the foxtrot and the tango."

Which still seemed pretty overwhelming. I glanced over at Calvin, but he was wearing his impassive face—which, after being with him for almost two years, wasn't as hard to read as it once might have been. I could tell that, although he wasn't entirely thrilled about the plan, he also wasn't going to get in the way.

Not when me going undercover as a competitor might make the difference between Archie staying a free man and spending the rest of his life in prison.

"All right," I said, knowing how reluctant I sounded. "Let's give Eddie a call and see if he's on board with this plan."

As I spoke, though, I couldn't help wondering whether I'd be more relieved if he agreed to dance with me...or if he didn't.

## 6

## Cheek to Cheek

IT TURNED OUT EDDIE BIXBY WAS thrilled at the thought of getting a last-minute partner to help him take a second crack at the Stepping Stars competition. Since I wasn't present during any of those phone calls, I didn't know exactly what Victoria said to him, but our first practice session was scheduled for early Tuesday evening, giving him time to drive in from Mesa, where he lived. I'd at first offered to be the one to drive to him, and Victoria and Archie shot down that idea pretty quickly, saying that they had the practice space at their house, whereas we would have had to find somewhere in Mesa. Since Eddie seemed fine with driving out to Globe, I'd decided the topic wasn't worth arguing any further.

But before I could head over to Archie and Victoria's house, Josie practically stalked into Once in a Blue Moon, her entire plump figure vibrating with indignation.

"Exactly *when* were you going to tell me?" she demanded, light blue eyes glinting with indignation, and I blinked at her. The shop was never very busy on weekday afternoons, and I'd been caught up in an awful daydream where I kept stepping on Eddie's toes until he declared me an utter disaster and said he was going to find a different replacement partner.

"Tell you what?" I said innocently. Of course, I knew exactly what she was talking about; the story of the murder at the Stepping Stars competition hadn't completely dominated the news, but it had been covered enough that I was sure Josie must have seen something about it.

"This mess with your cousin Archie," she snapped. That was almost always the way she described him, as though she thought I would never have associated with him in the first place if he wasn't a relative. Nothing could have been further from the truth, since Archie and I had been through a lot together and I now considered him the brother I'd never had, but I didn't bother to disabuse her of the notion. Josie thought what Josie wanted to think, and there was no point in trying to get her to budge on the topic.

"Oh," I said lamely. "Well, I didn't really want

to bother you with it—I know you were busy this weekend."

Again, nothing more than the truth. She'd made the mayoral decision to have a carnival in town over Memorial Day weekend, and making sure it all ran smoothly had taken up most of her time and energy. I knew she hadn't been too thrilled about Calvin and me leaving for Scottsdale rather than sticking around town and offering her moral support, but I'd only told her the truth, which was that we'd had the Stepping Stars competition on our calendars long before she'd even come up with the idea to have a carnival that same weekend, and that Archie and Victoria were counting on us to be there.

"Not busy enough to miss the way your cousin was accused of murder," Josie told me. A pause, and then she said, "He *is* innocent, right?"

"Of course he is," I replied, trying not to sound too indignant. "It's obvious someone is trying to frame him. I just have to figure out who that person is."

Now she looked a little less annoyed, and instead almost excited. "Oh, you're going to solve the crime?"

"I'm going to try," I said, then stopped there. While Josie would probably find out sooner rather than later about how I'd suddenly decided to enter the rescheduled competition—and make her own guesses as to why I would be doing something so completely out of character—I didn't see the need to tell her everything right now. "It's the least I can do for Archie."

A pause as I tried not to stare too pointedly at the clock on the wall above the cash register, which was currently telling me it was almost five and I needed to get the store locked up so I had enough time to take Sadie home before I headed over to Archie and Victoria's house. I'd let him leave early so he could be there in case Eddie showed up ahead of schedule, which meant I was responsible for making sure Once in a Blue Moon was closed up properly...and on time.

Josie didn't miss my glance, and said, "Well, I won't keep you. It *is* terrible about your cousin, though."

"It is," I agreed. "But I'm going to fix it."

Even as I uttered the words, however, I wondered if I was being just a little too optimistic.

---

When I got to Victoria and Archie's house, though, it was to find out that Eddie had texted Victoria to let her know he was running a little late but would be there by six. Annoyance flared, but I did my best to tamp it down. After all, he was driving here all the way from Mesa, and stuff happened.

Anyway, Calvin was working late that night, so I didn't have to worry about rushing home to make dinner after my dance practice. I'd brought Sadie to work with me that day because I didn't want to leave her alone for such a long stretch, and that meant she would be fine no matter how long my rehearsal with Eddie might go.

In fact, the dog was probably roaming around the large dog run we'd built for her, cheerfully stopping to sniff every blade of grass and bush, so I knew I didn't need to worry about her. She had a doggie door, meaning she'd be able to come and go as she wanted, and could head back inside whenever she decided she'd had enough fresh air.

No, right now I had much bigger things to worry about.

"We should talk about costumes while we're waiting for Eddie," Victoria said. We were sitting at her dining room table, since the open-concept living/dining/kitchen area was the first space she'd redone at the house. I had to admit it all looked lovely, from the wide-plank hickory floors to the dark beams overhead, not to mention the antique mantel she'd installed to replace the fireplace's former brick surround. Although I'd only been in the house once when it still belonged to Miriam Jacobsen, I remembered it as being fussy and traditional, looking like she'd bought every single piece from Ethan Allen so it would all match perfectly.

I tried not to sigh. Almost as soon as I agreed to this caper, I'd realized I would need to acquire at least one gown for the competition. While the thought hadn't exactly filled me with joy, I'd still tried to reassure myself it could have been worse. At least when doing the traditional dances, I wouldn't have to worry about wearing one of the skimpy gowns that seemed to be *de rigeur* for those competing in the Latin section of the contest.

"I'd loan you one of mine," Victoria went on. "But...."

She didn't complete the sentence, but she didn't need to. I maintained a pretty solid size six figure, but Victoria was definitely thinner than I was. There was no way in the world I'd be able to squeeze into one of her gowns.

"It's fine," I said hastily. "Can I commission something?"

"Not and have it in time for the competition," she replied at once. "The best dressmakers are booked up for months. But that's okay—we'll get you something secondhand."

"'Secondhand'?" I repeated, knowing I sounded way too dubious. True, back in the day, I'd loved hitting the various vintage and thrift stores around L.A., always looking for a treasure, but at the same time, I wasn't sure I liked the idea of wearing some other competitor's cast-offs.

Victoria smiled, telling me she knew exactly what I'd been thinking. "Oh, there's a big market for secondhand competition gowns," she told me. "They're very expensive, but at the same time, we dancers don't want to be seen in them too many times. So maybe we'll wear them once or twice—or possibly a little more than that—and then we have them professionally cleaned and put them up on a website that specializes in that kind of thing. We'll get you a dress from someplace close, like California or Texas, so it'll get here in plenty of time but still won't be anything that people in Arizona would have seen."

Clearly, she'd thought this through. I wondered if any of her own gowns had been bought on the secondhand market but thought it might be kind of gauche to ask.

Anyway, since it seemed pretty obvious I didn't have any other choice, considering the time constraints we were working with, I just said, "Okay—let's take a look."

Fifteen minutes later, I had two gowns on order—one a beautiful deep blue, and the other a dreamy rose pink—and I was returning my credit card to my purse. No, money wasn't really an issue, but I still hated to think what those dresses must have cost new, since even secondhand they still were selling for almost five hundred dollars each. Shoes would have been another issue, except that Victoria and I wore the same size, and she'd offered me a pretty pair of silver leather dance heels for me to wear, in addition to the simple black ones she'd given me to practice in.

During all this, Archie had been conspicuously absent. However, Victoria had told me he was busy polishing the floor down in the basement so it would be ready for whenever Eddie showed up, which provided a plausible excuse for why he'd made himself scarce. If that particular piece of busy work also meant he didn't have to be around while we two women were shopping for gowns, well, I supposed it worked out the best for all of us.

The doorbell rang then, and Victoria excused herself to go answer it. A moment later, she returned to the dining room, a tall man in a dress shirt and dark slacks a pace or two behind her.

"Selena, this is Eddie Bixby," she said, although I'd already guessed who he must be. "Eddie, this is my friend Selena Marx."

I got up from where I'd been sitting and extended a hand. "Very nice to meet you."

"Nice to meet you, too, Selena," he responded.

Maybe the look he gave me then was just a little too penetrating, although I told myself he was probably just sizing me up to see whether he thought I would make a respectable replacement partner for him. And on the surface, we did look like we would be pretty well matched—he had dark hair and blue eyes, just like I did, although his hair was more a mahogany brown than my near black, while my eyes had always hovered somewhere between blue and gray, not Eddie's bright sky color.

Still, on the surface, it seemed as though we would look fairly good together.

Well, at least until I started dancing.

"I appreciate you stepping in so I don't have to skip the competition," he went on, offering me a friendly smile. "I didn't think I was going to be able to find anyone on such short notice."

His words made me shoot a questioning glance at Victoria. I really hoped she hadn't led him on by promising I was some kind of expert. She sent me an encouraging nod, as if to tell me I could be as truthful as I wanted.

"Well, I don't have a lot of experience—" I began, but Eddie just shook his head, smile not wavering for a second.

"That's fine. We'll be competing with the rest of the novices." He stopped there and also looked over at Victoria. "But it probably would be a good idea for us to get started so I can see what I'm working with."

Uneasiness churned in my stomach. I certainly didn't measure my self-worth by how well I could dance the foxtrot—in other words, barely at all—but I still didn't want to look like a complete klutz.

Also, if Eddie decided I was beyond hope and it would be better for him to sit this one out rather than embarrass himself for all eternity, there went our plan of getting me up close and personal with the rest of the competitors...and any chance of discovering who had really killed Brad Masters.

"Sure," Victoria said. "Archie's waiting for us downstairs."

Maybe just the slightest flicker of unease crossed Eddie's features. True, the general belief was "innocent before proven guilty," but even so, I got the impression he wasn't thrilled to be spending time with an accused murderer. He must have been pretty desperate to stay in the competition if he was willing to overlook Archie's involvement in all this.

But since Eddie didn't say anything, Victoria led the two of us out of the dining room and down the stairs just off the kitchen, leading down to the basement.

This was the first time I'd ever been in the space, so I had no idea what it had looked like when Miriam owned the house. Now, though, the floors were covered in shining oak, and mirrors lined one wall. Another wall had been painted flat white and had a projector pointed toward it from a mount on the ceiling. A way for Archie and

Victoria to watch dance moves life-size while they were practicing?

I didn't know for sure, since I was definitely new to all this.

Archie had been standing at the far side of the room, behind a large table covered with lots of expensive-looking sound equipment. For the first time, I realized that speakers had been installed in the walls and ceiling, probably to provide a wash of sound no matter where you were standing.

*Victoria must've gotten a heck of a lot of money for her condo,* I thought as I tried to mentally calculate how much this setup must have cost. True, I hadn't asked how much below asking price their new house had sold for, nor had I ever pried about the couple's personal finances. Victoria had earned top dollar when running her event-planning business, but she was cutting back on that, and even though she'd done one or two small interior design jobs since earning her certification in March, it wasn't as if her new venture was fully up and running yet.

And even though I paid Archie a decent chunk of change to work in the store—more than most people would have thought was necessary—I knew it definitely wasn't enough to cover this kind of setup.

*None of your business,* I reminded myself. After all, the couple had won quite a few tournaments over the past few months, and even if none of those competitions had top prizes as big as the ones at the Stepping Stars contest, those prize earnings still weren't exactly what you could call insignificant, either.

"Hi, Archie," Eddie said, as if he knew he needed to act natural, no matter what his personal reservations about the situation might be. "This is quite the setup you have here."

"Thank you," Archie replied. "Although Victoria is the one who should get most of the credit, since she designed the space."

She shrugged. "Oh, it was pretty simple. It wasn't like I was designing a kitchen or a master suite or something. Anyway," she went on, voice turning brisk, "we might as well get started, right?"

I would have been just fine with prolonging the inevitable with as much small talk as possible, but I knew she was correct. "Sure," I said, and was glad to hear my voice didn't waver a bit.

Now I just had to hope I could fake it as easily on the dance floor.

"In this competition, we'll be doing the Viennese waltz," Eddie told me, his eyes narrowing just a little as I blinked.

What the heck was a Viennese waltz? Was that different from the box step Victoria had walked Calvin and me through when we were prepping for our wedding reception?

"You do know what that is, right?" Eddie asked.

"Sure," I lied. After all, how hard could it be?

That question was answered in the next couple of minutes as I realized the Viennese waltz was the beautiful, constantly spinning dance I'd watched Victoria and Archie perform all those times I'd attended their competitions. They made the whole process look completely effortless, of course, but the reality was that you needed to be quick on your feet and also always careful to avoid getting tangled up with your partner.

"Ouch," Eddie grunted after I stepped on him for the third time.

"Sorry," I said, and did my best to smile. "Guess my biorhythms are off today."

"You need to stop looking down," Archie said, after switching off the music. "You're trying to anticipate rather than going with the flow of the dance."

That sounded like the sort of advice I would have given a client when performing a Tarot reading, so hearing something so borderline woo-woo come from my oh-so-Virgo friend's mouth might have been amusing if the situation weren't so dire.

"He's right," Victoria chimed in. "Here—let's switch partners for a minute. Maybe it'll be easier for you to dance with someone you know."

Maybe...or maybe not. Dancing the Viennese

waltz involved allowing your partner to put his arm around your waist while you rested your left hand on his shoulder and he held your right hand in his left. It had felt odd enough doing that with Eddie, a man I'd only met some fifteen minutes earlier, but to have that kind of contact with Archie? Over the past year, we'd shared one or two extremely awkward hugs at the most, because I knew he wasn't a touchy-feely person and didn't enjoy those sorts of intimacies.

But coming out and admitting it would feel too weird to dance with Archie would only make the situation that much worse, so I told myself to suck it up. We were just dancing. People did it all the time with partners they weren't romantically involved with.

A pause while Victoria went over to the sound system and started up "The Blue Danube" once again, and then Archie put his hand on my waist and took my hand in his. There was something so no-nonsense about his stance that I found myself immediately relaxing. Clearly, he didn't seem worried about dancing with me, and that meant I needed to put my own doubts aside.

And after we started dancing, I realized Victoria had been right. Archie was a better dancer than Eddie, or at least, he appeared much better at compensating for my bobbles and missteps, to the point where I found myself relaxing and even having fun. There was something almost entrancing about the swirling movements of the dance, of having the room spin past as you floated along with the melody.

When the song ended, Archie gave a nod that was almost approving. "That was a definite improvement. Let's try the foxtrot next."

He spent the next half hour or so coaching me through that one, and then another forty-five minutes on the tango. I had to admit the tango was the hardest, not just because the rhythm of the dance felt so different, but because we were supposed to stare passionately into our partner's eyes as we performed the steps. There was no way in the world I would ever feel passionate about Archie, so half the time I made a mistake, it was due to my desperately attempting not to burst into a fit of the giggles.

Even so, at the end of the two hours, he seemed to think I was ready to switch back to dancing with Eddie, who'd been partnered with Victoria that whole time, and after Archie put us through our paces, I had to admit I was doing much better. Not anything close to competition-level, of course, but at least I was no longer tripping over my own feet... or my partner's.

Both Victoria and Archie seemed pleased with my progress, and since Calvin had already told me which nights he'd be working late the next couple of weeks, it was easy enough to set up the remainder of my practice sessions with Eddie. We'd get together five times in all, which didn't seem like enough.

However, Victoria reminded me that we'd be dancing in the novice division, and the two of us already looked better than a lot of the people who would be competing in that class.

"You're going to do great," she said, while Eddie smiled and I hoped she wasn't blowing the proverbial sunshine my way.

Then again, I wasn't competing to win. I was only doing this to gain access to the backstage area and get to know the other dancers, all the while hoping I might find a clue that would lead me to the real murderer. Not that I could admit such a thing to Eddie, who clearly thought he still had a chance at winning his division, despite being accompanied by a rank amateur like me.

Well, even if I had an ulterior motive for attending, I knew I'd still try my hardest not to embarrass him. He was doing me a huge favor—although he didn't know it—and I needed to do what I could to return that favor.

Whether it would be enough was entirely up for debate.

## 7

## Two Right Feet

THE NEXT TWO WEEKS PRACTICALLY FLEW by, somewhat to my surprise. Yes, there was the unpleasant business of Archie having to attend a preliminary hearing, where the judge ruled there was enough evidence to continue to trial—something we'd all been dreading but also knew was the most likely outcome—but otherwise, the days ticked by in an orderly fashion, broken here and there by my practice sessions with Eddie. We were getting better and better at moving together in harmony, and even though I wasn't sure I wanted to admit it to myself, I thought we might actually have a chance at placing in our division, although probably not taking the top prize.

One bit of excitement occurred when the gowns I'd ordered arrived, and I had to admit I did feel a little like Cinderella when I tried on the blue dress with the sparkly rhinestones on the bodice and then did a little twirl in front of the mirror in the bedroom I shared with Calvin. Luckily, he was at work and therefore not around to see me acting like a girl playing dress-up with her mom's evening wear, but still, seeing myself in the dress made me realize this was all actually going to happen, that in less than a week, I was going to be competing in the rescheduled Stepping Stars dancesport contest.

Because the resort had had to shoehorn the rescheduled competition into its calendar at the last minute, there hadn't been many hotel rooms to go around. That meant we'd all be driving in rather than staying, but as far as I was concerned, that was a good thing. At least I'd be able to sleep in my own bed those nights, and would only need my friend Hazel to watch Sadie during the day rather than around the clock.

On the other hand, staying at the resort would have given me more opportunities to see my fellow competitors interacting with one another. I tried to console myself by pointing out that most of them were going to be commuting from their homes as well, so I probably wouldn't be missing out on too much.

Hopefully.

And as much as I would have liked Archie to come along and be my guide and coach, we all agreed that wasn't a very good idea. So far, the police didn't seem to have made any headway in the case, although—two days before I would be entering the competition—Archie had told me the forensics people with the Scottsdale P.D. were finally done analyzing the steamer trunk and asked to return it to him. That surprised me a little, because I thought they would have needed to keep it until after his trial, but maybe they'd decided it didn't contain any useful evidence and wanted to get rid of the big, bulky item.

"And you said?" I asked, thinking I certainly wouldn't have wanted the thing back. The chances of the trunk being haunted by Brad Masters' ghost were probably pretty low, but....

"I told them they could dispose of it," Archie replied, with a twitch of his shoulders that was most likely him trying to hold back an obvious shudder. "Why in the world would I want it back? I certainly could never use it for storage after...well, after what happened."

No, probably not.

"Did the police have anything else to say?" So far, neither Archie nor Victoria had mentioned a single thing about when his trial would be scheduled, although I got the feeling there must have been some wrangling going on behind the scenes. Following some advice from Alec Scurlock, the San Ramon tribe's lawyer, Archie had hired a criminal defense attorney named Leland Bernstein, a man with an excellent record of keeping his clients out of prison. I had no doubt he'd do his best to make sure my friend remained a free man, but all the same, I knew I would work damn hard to make sure matters never got to that point.

"No," Archie replied. "We still don't have a trial date. Judging by a few things Eddie has told me, it sounds as though a lot of the other dancers don't think I had anything to do with it, but clearly, the deputy D.A. has a different view on the matter."

That didn't surprise me too much. True, the sensational stories on the local news had pretty much disappeared entirely, since no new details had come out regarding the case, and yet I had to believe the D.A. wanted a nice, tidy conviction and no loose ends. However, I was encouraged that Archie's fellow ballroom dancers didn't believe he could be behind such a grisly crime, and for a second or two, I wondered if it might be safe to have him come along to the competition after all.

As soon as that thought passed through my mind, however, I immediately shot it down. I'd have Victoria with me, after all, which meant I wouldn't be flying completely solo. Also, Calvin had made sure to schedule that weekend off so he could come along and lend additional moral support.

Better for Archie to stay here in Globe, far, far

away from the Stepping Stars contest. He'd already told me he'd watch the store in my absence on Saturday, and make sure to take a very public shopping trip at Walmart on Sunday so he'd have plenty of witnesses to verify his whereabouts just in case some skullduggery went down at the rescheduled competition.

That didn't seem very likely, although I couldn't dismiss the possibility out of hand, either. A much smaller tournament had taken place the weekend after Brad Masters was murdered, and it sounded as though the event had been completely ordinary in every way. Because of that, I had to believe Brad's death was a one-off occurrence, something that had been personally motivated... even if I had absolutely no idea what that motivation might have been.

"Well, that's good to hear about your dance friends," I said. "It shows that the people who really know you also know there's no way in the world you could have done anything like that."

He shrugged. "I suppose so. It's just frustrating that Victoria and I won't be able to compete. Until we achieve pro status, we're going to have a difficult time getting our dance studio going."

*It might also be a little difficult if your prospective clients all think you're a murderer,* passed through my head, but I wisely remained silent. The last thing I wanted was to torpedo Archie's dream of opening his own studio. I understood how important it was for him to have his own business, to not keep working at a job he looked on as charity and not something that was strictly necessary to keep the shop running.

I could have tried to disabuse him of that notion, but why? My store was rarely busy enough that two people needed to be working there, although it was nice to have Archie around so we could both have two days off each week. Before he'd taken on the position, I'd worked six days straight, only giving myself Sunday as a free day. Having him leave to manage his own dance studio wouldn't be the end of the world—I couldn't claim that running Once in a Blue Moon was exactly the most onerous job out there—but still, I'd already vowed to myself that I would try to hire someone part-time after he left so my schedule would have a bit more freedom in it.

There was also that other little matter, one Calvin and I hadn't discussed with anyone except each other. At New Year's, after we'd toasted the arrival of a brand-new year with champagne in front of the fireplace, we'd decided it was time. The very next week, I'd gone to the doctor to get my IUD removed, and after playing it safe for two months as we waited for the remnants of the hormones to get out of my system, we'd been trying our best to get pregnant. So far, I'd only been confronted by a single, sad pink bar on the pregnancy tests I'd taken, but we had to believe at some point, our little family would expand to include a baby, and that meant I definitely would have to get extra help at the shop before too long.

"There are other competitions coming up," I pointed out, but Archie didn't seem too reassured by that obvious fact.

"None of them are as prestigious as the Stepping Stars," he said with a sniff, and I'd decided to let it go.

And now, two days later, Calvin and Victoria and I were all driving in my Renegade so I could take my own crack at the competition. Honestly, I thought I would be just fine if I managed to avoid stepping on Eddie's toes or face-planting when he dipped me during the tango...and, of course, was able to track down the real killer, thanks to my newly unrestricted access to the tournament's goings-on backstage.

We didn't talk a lot on the drive; I could tell Victoria was preoccupied, probably not thrilled about having to leave Archie behind, even if she understood the reason why. And Calvin, bless him, had to have realized how stressed out his two companions were, and how it was probably better for him to play chauffeur and not try to ease the tension by passing the time with small talk.

Not that Calvin had ever been very good at that sort of thing, anyway.

---

The novice division's first heat was scheduled for ten o'clock, which meant we'd left Globe a little before eight in order to get to Scottsdale in plenty of time to find a parking place and hustle me backstage so I could get changed. My two gowns and an overnight bag stuffed with dance shoes, stockings, and an emergency makeup kit rested in the cargo area in the back of the vehicle, although Victoria had applied my "ballroom face" before we headed out this morning. I'd submitted to the procedure because I knew the heavy makeup was a necessary component of the costume, but my false eyelashes kept brushing against the lenses of the sunglasses I wore and seemed determined to drive me absolutely crazy long before we reached our destination.

Despite that minor annoyance, we made it to the resort without incident. Because the parking lot was absolutely packed, Calvin dropped Victoria and me off at the entrance nearest to the backstage area, promising to catch up with us later, after the first heat had been danced.

I didn't really like the idea, even as I realized it was necessary. Because the backstage at these competitions could get crowded if all the participants brought their own entourages along, the Stepping Stars organizers had decreed that each person could only have one assistant or coach with them. Eddie hadn't told me whether he was bringing someone or flying solo, or I might have tried to wheedle that extra spot for my husband, but as it was, I knew I needed to be glad that at least I could have Victoria along for moral support.

We followed the signs to a place where a series of long tables had been set out, with numbers designating each competitor's assigned spot for their personal belongings. Victoria had warned me not to leave anything valuable in such a readily accessible location, and therefore I'd already handed over my wallet and phone so she could carry them around in her purse and make sure they stayed safe.

As I set down the overnight bag I was carrying —Victoria had my gowns in their swathing of plastic laid across her arms—Eddie emerged from the crowd. He was already wearing his tails, telling me he must have gotten here a good bit earlier than we had. I wasn't too surprised, since he lived so much closer to the resort than I did.

No greeting, only an uncharacteristically concerned glance at the clock on the far wall of the room. "We only have fifteen minutes. Are you sure you're going to be ready in time?"

"Yes," I said at once, hoping my confidence

wasn't misplaced. "Victoria just has to help me into my dress, and then I'll be ready to go."

"Okay," he replied. He didn't look completely reassured, but he also hadn't tried to voice any further concerns. "I'll just hang here until you're ready."

I nodded, and Victoria led me to another part of the backstage area where makeshift dressing rooms had been set up. Because we'd gotten here a little later than I would have liked, most of the other dancers were already dressed and hanging around a table on the other side of the space, probably where Eddie and I would need to check in once we were ready to go.

Moving as quickly as I could, I got out of the jeans, flip-flops, and button-up sleeveless blouse I was wearing—Victoria had told me to avoid anything that needed to be pulled over my head, since doing so could spell catastrophe for my makeup and the heavy chignon augmented with false hair that rested at the nape of my neck—and had her help me into the blue dress, followed by the silver heels she'd loaned me. She'd also let me borrow a rhinestone necklace and dangly earrings, since my own funky collection of artisan-crafted and antique pieces wasn't exactly appropriate for the occasion.

Once I was all put together, she nodded in approval. "You look gorgeous," she said. "Calvin's eyes are going to pop out of his head when he sees you in this."

"Well, I hope not," I returned, even though I had to admit her praise had given me a little more confidence. "I kind of like his eyes where they are."

She grinned, and the two of us exited the dressing room and went over to the spot where Eddie was waiting for us. I thought I detected a flash of admiration in his expression, but when he spoke, he was all business. That must have been his way of showing his nervousness, because during the weeks we'd been practicing, he'd been nothing but friendly and low-key.

"We need to go check in," he said. "Then we can wait over there."

He nodded toward the group of other dancers who were clustered near the door. I didn't recognize any of them, but I supposed that wasn't so strange. Lately, I'd been paying much more attention to the open amateurs and the pros, since open amateur was the division Archie and Victoria occupied, and they hoped to soon turn professional.

However, after Eddie and I had signed in at the table where several volunteers were working, I still did my best to listen in to the various conversations taking place around us, even as I also tried very hard not to look as though I was eavesdropping.

And no, it wasn't as if I expected any of the people standing there to blurt out that they were responsible for Brad Masters' death, but at the same time, I thought I might pick up a tidbit that could help me in my search for the killer.

Unfortunately, everyone seemed to either be discussing finer points of technique, obviously trying to get those details fixed in their minds before they stepped out on the dance floor, or they were dealing with a case of the nerves, something I definitely could sympathize with. As many times as I tried to tell myself that it didn't matter how high I placed, and therefore I could let myself relax, those inner words of advice didn't appear to be doing me much good. My neck still felt way too tense, and a whole swarm of butterflies seemed to be fluttering around in my stomach.

Or maybe that was just my body's reaction to the tight bodice of my dress. In general, I didn't wear anything terribly form-fitting, and although it wasn't as though I was wearing a corset or something equally constricting, the gown did have some boning in it to give it structure, and wasn't what you could call exactly comfortable.

In fact, it felt as though one of those plastic bones wanted to keep poking me in the armpit no matter what I did.

"Everything all right?" Victoria asked, and I nodded.

"Sure," I lied, even as I thought that if I'd had

the time to get a truly custom gown, it probably would have fit me a lot better.

I didn't have the opportunity to worry about such minor annoyances, though, because one of the volunteers got up from the check-in table and announced, "It's time. Please go out to the dance floor and take your positions."

The butterflies in my stomach threatened to turn into a swarm of hornets, but I knew I couldn't surrender to my anxiety, even as I left Victoria behind and allowed Eddie to lead me out to the dance floor. His hand as he took mine felt warm and completely dry, so if he was having his own attack of the nerves, at least it wasn't manifesting as perspiration.

And I had to be glad that he'd done this plenty of times before, because he knew exactly where to lead me, taking me to the far end of the large wooden dance floor that had been set up in the auditorium. Bright lights blazed down from above, making it difficult to see the audience. That would have been a blessing, except I'd hoped I could find Calvin in the crowd and catch a glimpse of the encouraging smile I knew he must be wearing.

But all those people were nothing more than one dark, amorphous mass, so I did my best to refocus my attention on the dance floor and the man who still held my hand as we waited for the music to begin.

"It's going to be fine," Eddie said in an undertone. "You've really been killing it these past couple of days."

I did my best not to wince at the unfortunate choice of words. True, my dancing skills had improved much more rapidly than I'd thought they would, but considering I was only here to track down a murderer, I really wished he'd found a different way to praise my progress.

At least over the last few weeks, I'd allowed myself to get more comfortable with him, and even to think I might like him as a friend. As soon as he'd realized I was happily married, he'd dropped even the slightest hint of flirtation in his tone, and hadn't given me any more of those up-and-down looks that I'd found so uncomfortable during our first meeting. No, he seemed to look at the entire situation as a practical arrangement and nothing more, which I found comforting.

The music began then, and I didn't have time to think about anything else except following Eddie's lead as we swirled our way through "Tales from the Vienna Woods" and then moved on to "Dancing Cheek to Cheek." After the foxtrot came "Por Una Cabeza," our steps slowing down into the tango.

Through all of this, I did my best to focus only on the music and on Eddie's expert lead. True, I had an ulterior motive for being here, but if I didn't acquit myself well on the dance floor, then I might invite suspicion, might have people asking how I'd popped up out of nowhere merely to enter this competition. Yes, beginning dancers had to start somewhere, but they generally did so at smaller local events, not a big statewide contest like the Stepping Stars dancesport tournament.

To my infinite relief, I didn't stomp on my partner's feet or lose the rhythm. And even though I definitely didn't have any attention to spare on the people around us, I had to think I'd acquitted myself fairly well.

Judging by the triumphant smile on Eddie's face as the music ended and all of us on the dance floor took our bows, he clearly thought we'd done a bang-up job, a sentiment he uttered aloud once we'd headed backstage.

"You were amazing," he said, and I found myself blushing a little...or maybe my cheeks were just flushed from my recent exertions.

"So were you," I replied truthfully. "I just wish we didn't have to wait until tomorrow to find out how we really did."

"Oh, it'll go faster than you think," he replied. "We've got a lot of dance watching to do between now and then. Speaking of which, we should probably head out to the audience so we can watch the novice Latin heat."

Right—Eddie and I weren't competing in that

part of the event, but it was scheduled to take place at eleven, with a lunch break immediately following.

Just as we were turning to head toward the exit, Victoria emerged from the crowd of friends and assistants and instructors backstage, and hurried over to give me a quick hug.

"The two of you looked fabulous!" she exclaimed. "I wish Archie could have been here to see you."

I wished it, too, if only to show him how much his assistance had helped me to get to this point. Obviously, I'd practiced with Eddie, but if it hadn't been for Archie stepping in to help clarify a particular dance move or to articulate how I should be interacting with a certain song, I doubted I would have been able to acquit myself so well today.

"But I got it on video," Victoria went on, brandishing her rose gold iPhone. "So at least he'll be able to see it for himself. Oh, and Calvin sent me a text—he's in the center section about five rows back, and he saved three seats for us."

Better and better. I really hadn't wanted to abandon my two companions, but at the same time, I hadn't been sure whether my husband would be able to save that many seats when the auditorium was so crowded.

Then again, I didn't know how many people would want to argue with a guy who topped six foot five and looked like he could put them through a wall without breaking a sweat. Not that Calvin would ever do such a thing, of course, but I knew how deceptive appearances could be.

The three of us made our way out of the backstage area and into the audience. As we went, Eddie and I got some approving nods and even a couple of thumbs-ups, telling me Victoria wasn't the only one who thought we'd done well. I did my best to smile in return, not sure how to react to all the attention. Although I thought I tended to be fairly equally balanced between introvert and extrovert, I still wasn't the type to put myself out there. The only reason I was doing any of this was to help Archie, and I couldn't wait to fade back into comfortable obscurity.

Eddie, on the other hand, obviously was used to this sort of thing, because he smiled at our well-wishers and waved and returned the thumbs-ups as we climbed up the bleachers to get to the spot where Calvin was sitting. We probably would have been less conspicuous if we'd been able to change back into our street clothes before heading into the audience, but it wasn't as easy to switch outfits with our current setup, since I didn't have a hotel room to retreat to in order to make the change, and Victoria had told me it was traditional to have on some kind of evening wear throughout the competition.

Tradition or not, my oversized ballgown wasn't exactly a good fit for the folding chairs that had been set out on the risers, and I had to sort of scrunch myself to fit. A couple of royal blue feathers floated on the air during this procedure, and Calvin grinned at me, even as he leaned over to tell me how great Eddie and I had looked during our performance.

"You were definitely the best," he concluded, and I shook my head.

"You might just be a little biased, sweetheart."

His smile didn't fade. "True...but I also have 20/20 vision."

I couldn't dispute that fact. Honestly—aside from his pretty awful seasonal allergies—Calvin was definitely a flawless physical specimen, up to and including his perfect eyesight.

"Well, here's hoping the judges feel the same way," Victoria put in after hearing our exchange.

"Oh, I'm pretty sure they do," Eddie said.

I wasn't sure I shared his confidence, but then again, he'd competed in plenty of tournaments and probably had a much better idea of what the judges were looking for than I did.

Anyway, the emcee approached his podium and announced that the novice dancers' Latin portion of the competition was about to begin, which meant we all needed to quiet down as the participants made their way onto the floor.

Watching them, I could see why Archie was reticent about competing in this division of a ballroom dance tournament. I'd teased him a while back about wearing a sequined spandex jumpsuit, and I hadn't been too far off the mark. While he was in great shape and would probably look just fine in even the most outlandish costume, his modesty would have a hard time dealing with that kind of display.

Could he even run a studio if he didn't have experience with those sorts of dances?

I reassured myself that just because he didn't want to compete in those divisions, it didn't mean he wasn't well-acquainted with the rumba and samba, the salsa and merengue. Why tango wasn't included in that group, since it seemed just as Latin as the others, I wasn't sure, but maybe it was an older dance and therefore had been lumped in with the waltz and the foxtrot.

Something I needed to ask Victoria about... when I had the chance.

For the moment, though, I remained silent as I watched the novice group go through their paces. Some of them were really good, and I guessed they'd be moving up to the open amateur division soon enough. At the same time, I could only be grateful that Eddie and I had stuck to the traditional dances and hadn't ventured out into Latin realms. There was no way in the world I could have mastered the steps the dancers were performing—definitely not in the space of two weeks, and maybe not ever.

Luckily, I hadn't been required to do anything that advanced, so it was enough just to watch and wonder which couple the judges would decide had taken first place. There were two who seemed equally matched to me—a dark-haired pair in striking coral and silver costumes, and a man and woman who looked a little older than a lot of the other competitors, and who wore black and gold.

There were also some people who seemed to be having a hard time keeping up, and made missteps that even an amateur like me could spot immediately.

Well, it was the novice group. I couldn't really expect everyone to be competing on the same level.

And I also had to wonder if I'd looked as obviously out of my element as those dancers I saw on the floor now.

Because all the winners wouldn't be announced until the end of the following day, it did feel a little anticlimactic as the pairs left the dance floor and the emcee returned to the podium to announce the lunch break and to say the competition would resume at one-thirty, with a "mixer" following the afternoon heats. Also, I couldn't help but feel as if I hadn't accomplished very much today. I was supposed to be here tracking down the person—or persons—who'd killed Brad Masters, but so far I hadn't found a single actionable clue.

*Rome wasn't built in a day,* I reminded myself as Calvin and I and our companions got up from our chairs.

No, it wasn't. But if I couldn't discover the killer's true identity before this whole thing went to trial, Archie had a good chance of ending up in prison for the rest of his life.

I knew I would never let that happen...no matter what.

## 8

## All in the Mix

I HADN'T REALLY KNOWN WHAT WE WOULD do for lunch—the resort had three restaurants, and yet there was still no way in the world everyone attending the tournament would fit into them—but I should have known I could rely on my friend Victoria's resourcefulness. It turned out she'd made reservations at the hotel's café just as soon as the competition was rescheduled, so the four of us were able to slide into a corner booth even as we got the evil eye from other attendees who hadn't been so foresighted.

"I didn't think this place took reservations," Eddie said as Victoria passed around the menus the hostess had handed her.

"It doesn't," she replied serenely. "But I pulled a few strings. Anyway, we should order before this place completely fills up and the kitchen gets overloaded."

That sounded like a good idea. While I was hungry enough to munch my way through a burger, I wasn't sure whether my tightly fitting gown would appreciate that kind of indulgence.

Instead, I settled on a grilled chicken sandwich and a side salad, while Calvin, who obviously didn't have any wardrobe constraints to worry about, ordered the burger I'd been coveting. Eddie also got a cheeseburger, while Victoria, possibly sympathizing with me, requested the grilled chicken salad.

Once that was all settled, the conversation moved on to the afternoon's competition. "You should see some pretty amazing dancing," Victoria told me. "It'll be very inspiring."

I managed a wan smile. Right then, I only wanted to be "inspired" to head back to Globe, but I knew I needed to stick this out. Problem was, since Eddie knew nothing about my real reason for competing in the tournament, I couldn't comment on how I hadn't found a single actionable piece of evidence so far, or how I was thinking maybe this whole thing had been a huge mistake.

No, I had to pretend I was eager to dive into the world of competitive ballroom dancing and learn every single thing about it that I could.

"I'm really looking forward to it," I said. "And to the mixer. That sounds like fun."

My comment earned me a knowing glance from Calvin, who'd probably realized the only reason I was interested in the mixer was because it would afford the best opportunity for picking up some helpful clues. As my spouse, he could attend, but he'd already assured me he planned to hang back and let me do my thing.

Just as well. If the two of us had tried to dance together, I would only have proven how woefully inexperienced I was at all this. Eddie made me look good, but I wasn't going to fool myself into thinking I was now the next incarnation of Ginger Rogers or something.

But at least the conversation remained light, with Eddie saying he definitely would be moving out of the novice section if the two of us placed in the competition. Then he shot me an apologetic look.

"I hope you don't mind me bailing on you," he said.

I couldn't help smiling. "No, of course not," I responded. "I know you're just dancing with me because your regular partner is injured. It's not as if I expected this to be anything but temporary."

At once, he relaxed against the back of the booth. "Thanks for understanding," he said. "But I can help you find a new partner if you want."

"That's fine," I said quickly. "Right now, I'm not even sure if I want to compete on a regular basis. I kind of just wanted to see what all this was like."

Was that a flicker of disappointment in his bright blue eyes? "Oh, you shouldn't walk away just yet," he said. "You have a lot of potential."

While part of me wanted to tease him about the "potential" comment—what, he didn't think I was doing all right here and now?—I knew he was only trying to be sincere. "Thanks," I replied, doing my best to keep my mouth from twitching in amusement. Next to me, Calvin lifted his own glass of water and drank, probably in an attempt to do the same thing. "I appreciate that."

"You do have a lot of potential," Victoria said crisply. "But competing takes a lot of time and energy, so I completely understand if you're not sure you want to go on with all this."

I sent her a grateful look, even as Calvin said equably, "Well, no one has to make a decision right now. We can get through the weekend and see what happens, and then go from there."

That sounded like excellent advice. The waiter came back with our food then, and we abandoned the conversation for a while so we could eat our meals—quickly, because there was a long line of people waiting for tables, and it didn't seem fair for us to linger and deny some other group a chance to grab lunch before it was time to head back to the auditorium for that afternoon's heats.

As Victoria had said, there was a lot to watch and learn...not the least of which was the surprising sight of Joanna Greer, Brad Masters' former partner, heading out onto the dance floor for the traditional section of the open-amateurs part of the program. Her flaming red hair was too distinctive to ignore, especially contrasted with the lime-green ballgown she wore. The man at her side was a stranger—no big surprise—a tall guy with sandy hair and the air of someone not sure if they were exactly where they wanted to be.

"Who's that?" I whispered to Victoria, who sat next to me, Eddie on her other side.

"Tyler Simms," she replied at once. "He's been dancing open amateur for a while, but he kind of bounces from partner to partner. I guess it's not too surprising that Joanna might have latched on to him. I doubt it'll last, but she probably saw it as a chance to still earn some prize money despite just losing her partner."

I nodded, but because the music had begun right then, I figured it probably wasn't a good idea to keep chatting. Instead, I leaned forward slightly, concentration fixed on Joanna and her new partner, even though there were at least a dozen other couples also occupying the dance floor.

Obviously, she had to put on her game face to

be here, but at the same time, she certainly didn't look to me like someone who was grieving the loss of a murdered partner. Her chin was up, and a faint smile touched her red-glossed lips.

However, even though she and Tyler danced beautifully, I could tell they weren't quite in sync with one another, that a few times they were obviously off the beat during the foxtrot. They recovered, of course, but I had to believe that if I'd noticed, then the judges must have detected those bobbles as well.

And clearly, she wasn't too thrilled by hers and Tyler's performance, because her smile disappeared the second they exited the dance floor, and although I obviously couldn't hear a word they were saying, it sure looked to me like the couple exchanged a few heated words before they disappeared backstage.

"That didn't go too well," Victoria murmured. "Joanna would've been better off waiting for the next competition so she'd have more time to practice with her new partner."

No surprise that Victoria, who had much more experience in this sort of thing than I did, would have noticed right away how Joanna and her partner weren't vibing very well with each other.

"Maybe she needed the money?" I suggested, and Victoria shrugged.

"Maybe," she allowed before adding, "although

I don't know too many people who rely completely on their prize winnings to get by. In the grand scheme of things, it really isn't all that much. Most competitors have full-time jobs and just use the prize money on costumes and travel expenses, that kind of thing."

My friend's words really didn't come as too much of a surprise, not when I knew Eddie worked for a Toyota dealership in Mesa. With his glib good looks and friendly manner, he probably sold a lot of cars. At the same time, though, I had to wonder why Joanna would jump back into competing so soon after her partner's death if money wasn't the motivating factor. If Brad had been her husband or boyfriend in addition to her dance partner, then maybe I could have interpreted her presence at the competition this weekend as a way of trying to bury her grief by staying busy.

But everything I'd heard from Victoria had made it sound as if they weren't romantically involved, although my friend had been quick to add that she did her best not to pry into the other dancers' personal lives. Something here didn't appear to be adding up, although for the moment, I couldn't think what it might be.

I had to settle for giving a resigned lift of my shoulders, mostly because whatever was going on here, we definitely weren't going to figure it out without a lot more information than we currently possessed.

There was a fifteen-minute intermission between the two tracks, not really enough time to do anything much beyond stretching your legs or making a brief trip to the restroom. Even though I halfway needed to go, I decided to wait, partly because I knew there would probably be a horrendous line, and partly because I didn't feel like wrestling with my dress while in a hurry. After the dance competition ended at five, things would be a lot more relaxed, since all the spectators would go home and only the competitors and their plus-ones would remain behind.

Once the break was over, the dancers returned to the floor. And once again, I found myself watching Joanna Greer the closest, even though I doubted she and her partner had much of a chance of placing, thanks to their lackluster performance in the first half of the program. She wore her signature lime green, this time in a heavily beaded short dress that covered just enough of her to be barely legal.

Well, her dancing might be suffering because of the loss of her partner, but I had to admit she had truly spectacular legs.

And I didn't know what words of encouragement she and Tyler had shared during that short intermission, but something must have happened, because they seemed to be on fire this go-'round. If there were any missed steps or problems with keeping up with the music, my inexperienced eyes sure didn't see them. No, as far as I could tell, their performance in the Latin multi-dance seemed pretty much inspired.

Whether it would be enough to make up for their gaffes in the first part of the competition, I honestly didn't know. The two portions were judged separately, and yet, the goal of everyone competing was to win both divisions in order to capture the biggest chunk of prize money.

Still, maybe Joanna would be happy with only winning one section, especially so soon after losing Brad and having to train with an entirely new partner. I didn't know her at all, so I had no idea what outcome she'd been hoping for when she entered the tournament.

But maybe I'd get the opportunity to bump into her at the mixer, and would then have a chance to find out what she was really like.

*Don't get your hopes up,* I thought. True, we were all competing in the same contest, but she was one of the top-ranked open amateurs, while I was a nobody novice who'd only just entered her very first tournament. The chances that Joanna Greer would lower herself to talk to someone like me seemed pretty low.

You never knew, though, which was why I

reminded myself that I needed to keep my mind open so I'd be receptive to whatever the universe chose to throw my way.

But with the open amateurs' part of the competition finished for the day—Sunday morning's contests would be for the youth and senior divisions, with a country-western competition immediately following lunch and then an awards ceremony to take place half an hour after that ended—it was time for the auditorium to empty out and for the competitors and their companions to head over to the ballroom where the mixer would take place.

Honestly, it took all my devotion to Archie to compel me to walk over there with Calvin and Victoria and Eddie. If it weren't for my desperate need to clear Archie's name, I would have gone back to the dressing room and peeled myself out of that uncomfortable dress, then put on a skirt, tank top, and sandals, and headed straight back to Globe.

But as much as I would have liked to make my escape, I realized running away wasn't an option. Maybe I'd leave the mixer empty-handed, and yet I knew I could never face Archie if I didn't make the attempt.

So, even though my feet hurt and that darn piece of boning in my dress was probably leaving a lovely welt under my arm, I lifted my chin and headed into the ballroom.

At least there was a cash bar. All four of us made a beeline in that direction, Calvin because he probably needed a drink even more than I did, and Victoria and Eddie because they must have been able to tell that my husband and I needed a little bit of liquid courage to get through the next hour or so.

Once I had a glass of pinot grigio in my hand and Calvin had a beer—and Victoria a white wine spritzer and Eddie a gimlet—I felt a little more ready to relax into my surroundings. I had to admit the ballroom looked very festive, with *faux* palm trees flanking the DJ's station and tropical-themed flower arrangements on all the tables. Silk trees strung with white fairy lights stood sentinel against the walls, and really, with all the women in their bright ballgowns and sequined competition dresses standing around, the place looked a little like someone had spilled a bunch of bejeweled Christmas ornaments into the middle of the room.

I didn't see Joanna Greer anywhere, but consoled myself that she would probably be along shortly. Although the organizers hadn't said attendance at the mixer was mandatory, they'd also made it sound as though everyone was expected to put in some face time if they wanted to make a good impression.

When I turned back toward Calvin and Eddie and Victoria after completing my survey of the room, it was to see a man I didn't know, tall and thin and with the kind of lean, intense features that were arresting rather than handsome, talking to Eddie. The stranger also wore white tie and tails, telling me he was also a fellow competitor, although I didn't recognize him.

"You were great," the man was saying. His gaze strayed toward me, and he added, "The both of you. First time?"

That question was clearly directed toward me, since Eddie had been a fixture on the scene for the past couple of years, even if he hadn't achieved open amateur status yet, while I was clearly a newcomer.

"Yes, first time," I replied. "But I've been wanting to try this for a while."

A gentle fib, one I didn't think would get me in too much trouble. If I wanted to be entirely truthful with myself, I really had enjoyed the little dance lessons Victoria had given Calvin and me to get us ready for our wedding reception, and it was sort of disappointing to realize my future husband wasn't going to be spinning me around a ballroom Fred and Ginger–style any time soon.

But because Calvin possessed so many other sterling qualities, I couldn't exactly fault him for not being a ballroom king. Maybe, just maybe, if

Archie got his studio up and running, I could convince Calvin to take a few lessons with me. Not so we could compete, of course, but just so we could go out dancing every once in a while. Who knew? If everything went well, then possibly I could look into getting some kind of a club going in Globe, considering how it was definitely a pain to have to drive into Gilbert or Mesa any time we wanted to do anything remotely social. Maybe there really wouldn't be enough interest to support that sort of venture, but it still was probably worth investigating.

However, none of those rosy-hued dreams were going to happen if I couldn't figure out who had chopped Brad Masters into pieces and stuffed him into Archie's steamer trunk.

"Well, you did great," the stranger said, and extended his hand. "I'm Peter—Peter Tillis."

"Selena Marx," I responded. "And this is my husband, Calvin Standingbear."

The two men shook hands, and then Peter's gaze slid past Calvin's broad shoulder to the spot where Victoria was standing nearby, trying not to appear too awkward.

"I'm sorry about Archie," Peter said, and he did look honestly sympathetic as he addressed her. "If it's any consolation, I think the police are way off base on this whole thing."

Victoria's expression, which had appeared

fairly tense despite the couple of sips of white wine spritzer she'd just drunk, eased a little bit. "Thank you," she replied. "It's good to know that people aren't believing the worst."

"No," Peter said, and then a lopsided grin touched his thin lips. "If they would just understand that Archie was the kind of guy to freak out if he got a piece of lint on his jacket, then they'd realize he's pretty much the last person who'd be capable of doing anything like that."

I could tell Victoria didn't much like the "freak out" comment, because one brow lifted slightly before she caught hold of herself. However, it also seemed fairly obvious that she agreed with the content of Peter's remark if not the manner of its delivery, because she said, "I know. We've been trying and trying to tell them that the whole thing is completely out of character for Archie, even if he might have had a motive. Which he didn't." She stopped there and let out a breath, expression turning rueful. "But the police want everything wrapped up in a nice little bow, so they're just focusing on him instead of trying to figure out who else might have had the motive—and the means— to do such a horrible thing."

Peter shook his head. "It's a mess," he replied. "But I just wanted you to know that most of us are pulling for him."

I couldn't help noticing how Peter had said

"most" and not "all," but I supposed that was to be expected. Even if the overwhelming majority of the people in Arizona's ballroom-dance community believed Archie was innocent, there would still have to be a few who weren't yet convinced, or who simply didn't like him and therefore were all too glad to see him in such an awful position.

"And I appreciate that," Victoria said. She paused for a moment, then added, clearly trying to steer the conversation toward a topic that was a little less problematic, "So...what do you do when you're not ballroom dancing?"

He hitched his shoulders and gave us all a deprecating smile. "Oh, I work in the automotive industry."

"Like Eddie?" I asked, noticing how he'd moved away from our little group and was talking with several women in gowns even more elaborate than mine.

Trolling for a new partner? The mixer seemed like it would be the right venue for that kind of activity, and it made some sense. Neither one of us expected to keep dancing together indefinitely.

"Nope," Peter replied. "He's in new-car sales. I do auto restorations."

"Vintage cars?" Calvin inquired. My husband wasn't car-obsessed like a lot of men, but I could tell he was trying to be polite.

Peter nodded. "Right now I'm working on a

'40 Mercury coupe. Gorgeous car. The paint was a mess because it's been sitting in a barn on someone's ranch for the past fifty years or so, but the body is straight, and there's no rust because it's an Arizona car." He paused there, looking a little sheepish. "Sorry for the info dump. Once I get started talking about cars, it's hard to get me to stop."

"It's fine," I assured him. While I also wasn't much of a car buff, the passion in Peter's voice as he talked about his latest project was obvious, and I always liked to hear people expound on the topics that truly interested them. Also, my brain was already ticking away, processing his words. Archie seemed mostly content with the VW Beetle convertible I'd gifted him when I bought my Renegade, but what if I could have Peter track down something more his style, something like a car he might have driven back in the day before he was turned into a cat?

After all, a '55 Chevy convertible would make an awesome birthday present...assuming, of course, that Archie hadn't been found guilty of Brad Masters' murder before then.

*You'll figure it out,* I assured myself, even as yet another tremor of unease passed through me. I wanted to believe that, but...

...but since I didn't have a single piece of

evidence to work with, I didn't know how successful I'd be this time around.

"Anyway," Peter went on, "that's what I do. Some of the guys at the shop give me a hard time about the whole ballroom dance thing, but I really like it. Gives me a chance to do something completely different, you know?"

"Yes, I know," I said, even as I wondered if there were any hobbies that might attract my own interest in the same way. True, I had my Tarot cards and my crystals and my pendulums, but I considered working with them as just another part of my spiritual practice, not a hobby like woodworking or painting or snowboarding.

Then again, you could make a living at all those things if you were good enough, making them much more than a simple avocation. And while Once in a Blue Moon was technically my business, I didn't have to worry about it turning a profit. It used to, before I hired Archie full-time and made sure to get him insurance, but now the situation was entirely different.

Not that it mattered. I didn't need the money. At the same time, though, I wondered if I should start doing Tarot readings again, like I once did when I lived in L.A. I did them for myself all the time, of course, but that wasn't quite the same thing as performing a reading for someone else.

Every once in a while, I'd lay out the cards for a friend, like the time Hazel had asked me whether she should sell her house or keep it as an Airbnb. Maybe it would be fun to do that on a limited basis, just a few readings a week to keep me in top form.

Well, I'd think about that later, once this whole mess with Archie was resolved. Until then, I knew I needed to devote as much of my time as possible to tracking down whoever had killed Brad Masters.

Calvin had been wearing a slight smile through this entire exchange, telling me he probably thought Peter liked the whole ballroom-dance thing because it gave him a chance to partner with pretty women...although I didn't see anyone nearby who looked as though she might be his companion, and I couldn't remember seeing him on the dance floor with someone.

"Is your partner here?" I asked, and a faint hint of pink appeared in his thin cheeks.

"Um...I don't think so," he said, and scanned the crowd briefly. "Anyway, we decided after this competition that we'd go our separate ways."

"Oh, that's too bad," I replied, and once again he shrugged.

"It's fine. We were both thinking we weren't that compatible anyway."

I supposed that happened, and better to figure it out before you'd spent years and years with a partner. Or at least, I assumed that was the case here. Trying to figure out someone's age was always tricky, but Peter looked like he was probably around my age, so in his early thirties. I'd heard that some dancers started when they were just children, although I had to believe that wasn't the case here, not when he was still dancing in the novice category.

"Anyway," he went on, "it was nice to meet you. Tell Archie we're all rooting for him."

I murmured a thank-you, and then Peter moved off through the crowd, looking as though he was headed toward the refreshment table.

"He seems nice," I told Victoria, who'd edged closer once it was obvious my conversation with Peter Tillis was over.

She looked in the direction he'd disappeared, and tilted her head a little. "Yes, he does. Archie and I haven't interacted with him much because we've been dancing in different divisions, but it's good to know that most people don't think I'm engaged to an axe murderer."

Her tone made me think she was joking, if just a little bit. The reports made it pretty clear that Brad had been stabbed first and then hacked up later, although the final autopsy results hadn't been released yet, and therefore none of us really knew what kind of weapon had been used to whack off his limbs in order to make him fit in that steamer trunk.

"And if they do think that, they don't know Archie very well," Calvin observed.

That was for sure. I lifted my glass of wine to take a much-needed swallow of pinot grigio, even as I wondered how much face time we'd really need to put in at the mixer before we could all head back to Globe. Most of the people attending the event probably lived in the greater Phoenix area, but the three of us had a long drive home.

Just as I was about to ask Victoria how much longer we'd need to linger here, another dancer came up to me, a man not much taller than I and with a distinctly predatory gleam in his eye as he smiled and extended a hand. "Hi, I'm Ron Williams. You were pretty spectacular out there today."

"Um, thanks," I managed, even as I felt rather than saw Calvin moving a little closer to me. Then I realized a first-time dancer should probably appear a little more enthusiastic, and quickly added, "Being able to dance at Stepping Stars is like a dream come true."

Despite the near-foot difference in their heights, Ron didn't seem too intimidated by my husband's proximity. Still wearing that near-leer of a smile, he replied, "Well, you're pretty amazing on the dance floor. If things don't work out between you and Eddie, just let me know."

He produced a business card from his inside

breast pocket and handed it over. Feeling a little dazed, I went ahead and took it. Somehow, I made myself thank him, and stammer something about not being sure about my next step...no pun intended.

To my relief, though, he didn't press the issue, and wandered away after that, apparently satisfied now that he'd made his advance. Victoria, having watched this whole exchange, only shook her head.

"Ron's always trolling for partners," she said. "I'm sure he would have tried to give you something more than a business card if Calvin hadn't been here."

"Just doing my job, ma'am," he said with a grin, and I went up on my tiptoes so I could give him a quick kiss on the cheek.

"And thank the Goddess for that."

We all paused there, though, because Joanna Greer and her partner had finally made their delayed appearance. She still wore that shockingly short bright green beaded dress, but she didn't seem at all self-conscious as she accepted the greetings—and the condolences, I guessed—of the people who clustered around her, making her entrance seem more like that of a celebrity entering an upscale club rather than just another dancer showing up late to a not-quite-mandatory mixer.

Ron Williams approached her at once, and she just shook her head and kept going, as if he'd made his pitch to her multiple times and she wasn't in the mood to hear it again. And I thought I spotted Peter Tillis going up to her and saying something, although the two of them were far enough away that I couldn't hear what he said. She smiled at him, but her expression looked a little too tight to me, as though she knew she needed to act amiable even if she really wasn't in the mood.

Or maybe I was imagining things. I was tired, my feet hurt, my dress kept poking me, and I just wanted to go home. It was entirely possible that my brain had decided to manufacture things that weren't there because I was so physically uncomfortable.

To my relief, though, Victoria told us a few minutes later that we'd made our appearance, and so we could head for home.

*Thank the Goddess,* I thought as we headed out of the ballroom and over to the backstage area where the overnight bag with my street clothes waited. Two security guards were roaming around, keeping an eye on things, telling me the resort didn't intend to take any more chances with its dancers or their personal belongings.

*Kind of like shutting the barn door after the horses have escaped,* passed through my mind as I collected my bag and hurried over to one of the makeshift dressing rooms so I could change out of that damn dress. It was beautiful, but as far as I was concerned, it was going right back on that dance clothing barter site. I knew there was no way in the world I could cope with another day of having it poking holes in my armpit.

Soon enough, though, I was back in one of my infinitely more comfortable sequined skirts, along with a tank top and flat sandals. And despite it being nothing more than an extremely elegant torture device, I'd carefully hung up the dance dress and swaddled it in plastic, ensuring it should survive the drive home relatively unscathed.

Not long after that, we were headed back to Globe, with Calvin behind the wheel and Victoria occupying the back seat. I wasn't looking forward to doing this all over again tomorrow, even though I knew Sunday shouldn't be quite so onerous. Eddie and I wouldn't have to compete, after all, and the day would be over once the awards ceremony wrapped up at a little past four.

Even so, I couldn't quite ignore the doubt creeping through me, the feeling that all this had been for nothing. No little intuitive bursts to point me toward the killer, no one jumping up to the podium to proclaim they were the one who'd murdered Brad Masters.

Clearly, this was going to be a lot harder than I'd thought.

## 9

## A Major Award

I WAS FEELING GRUMPY WHEN I ROLLED out of bed the next morning, even though we didn't have to be back in Scottsdale as early as we had the day before. Because Eddie and I weren't performing and didn't really need to make an appearance until the big group dance that afternoon, I could be a bit more leisurely about my preparations, since we didn't have to even get on the road until after lunch.

"You're very quiet today," Calvin observed as we drove over to pick up Victoria at the house she and Archie shared.

"I'm tired," I replied. Normally, I didn't make those sorts of admissions, because life in general agreed with me and it took a lot to tucker me out. But even though I'd gotten a good, solid eight hours of sleep, I still felt draggy despite the multiple cups of tea I'd consumed so far that day.

Most likely, it was just the aftermath of spending so much time in crowds and in a high-energy sort of environment like the competition. I wouldn't say I was a true introvert, but I still liked my alone time and in general tried to avoid doing anything that involved being around large crowds of people I didn't know, which was pretty much the exact opposite of attending the Stepping Stars tournament.

"It's a lot, I agree," Calvin said, and sent a quick glance in my direction before returning his attention to the road. "But it'll all be over after today."

"Will it?" I asked, knowing how plaintive I sounded. "I mean, I'm spending all this time and energy—and dragging you along with me—but for what? I didn't learn anything of any use yesterday."

For a second or two, he didn't reply, but kept driving while he seemed to ponder my words. Then he said, "You don't know that for sure, Selena. That is, I've seen you work away at other murder cases, and a lot of the time, something that doesn't make sense at first is what finally helps you solve the mystery."

While I might have liked to argue with that particular observation, deep down, I knew he was right. I was no Sherlock Holmes, didn't use deductive logic to track down a murderer. Instead, I gathered lots of little bits of information and then let them churn away deep in a part of my brain I didn't fully understand. Eventually, the answer came to me—often backed up by the perpetrator also figuring out that I was on to them and doing their best to take me out—but trying to force it never, ever worked.

Maybe Archie had realized the same thing, or maybe Victoria had told him I was really going out on a limb with this whole undercover ballroom dance thing, but when I went to the door of the house the two of them shared while Calvin waited in the car, my friend looked cheerful enough as he opened it to greet me.

"Victoria will be down in just a minute," he added. "Can I get you some water or anything?"

"No, that's fine," I told him. Calvin and I had filled our travel cups out of the pitcher of filtered water at home, and I was good for now.

Archie nodded, then said, "She showed me the video from the competition. You and Eddie did well."

Because I knew Archie was not the sort of person to offer praise unless you'd really earned it, a happy little flush went through me at those words of approval. "We had good teachers," I replied.

"Maybe," he allowed. A sly grin tugged at his mouth as he added, "However, I highly doubt your husband would have done as well even with twice the instruction."

That traitorous thought might have passed through my own mind, even though I really didn't want to acknowledge it. Instead, I said, "You're saying he's hopeless?"

"No one is 'hopeless,'" Archie returned. "I'm only saying he'd need a lot more instruction to get him to the same place."

Victoria came down the stairs then, apologizing for keeping me waiting. Today she wore another cocktail gown, this one in a color somewhere between silver and champagne that looked quietly gorgeous with her blonde coloring. As for me, I once again planned to get changed at the event so I wouldn't wrinkle my ballgown.

With any luck, this one wouldn't spend the entire afternoon trying to stab me in the armpit.

She kissed Archie goodbye, and the two of us hurried down the front walk to the Jeep, which Calvin had kept running. Even in Globe, the day was way too hot to sit in a car with no air conditioning.

But soon enough, we were pulling away from the curb and headed west on the highway toward Phoenix. "Archie seemed like he was in good spirits today," I ventured.

Although Victoria was again sitting in the back seat, I still caught a glimpse of her nod in the rearview mirror. "He was really glad to see how well you and Eddie did," she said. "I think it helped him believe this idea of opening a dance studio isn't a pipe dream. Also, I told him what Peter said yesterday about most of the dancers not believing for a second that he could have committed such a terrible crime. Archie isn't the kind of person who makes friends easily—"

*You don't say,* I thought, although I held my tongue.

"—and I don't think he was really expecting that kind of support. So, even though all this has been really rough on him, knowing that the ballroom dance community is on his side makes a big difference."

It had made a big difference to me, too. Even though I understood the burden of ferreting out the real culprit rested pretty much squarely on my shoulders—mostly because I knew Detective Murphy sure as hell wasn't going to go out on a limb and start looking for another suspect when he had one right where he wanted him—I had to believe that public opinion must count for something. If nothing else, it might help influence the jury when this whole mess went to trial.

Not that I wasn't really, really hoping I'd get everything fixed well before then.

The parking lot at the resort was nearly as crowded as it had been the day before, but because

I wasn't performing and we'd all had lunch before we got on the road, I was feeling a lot less pressure today.

Well, pressure about dancing, anyway. I had to hope that maybe, since I wasn't so distracted with worries about tripping over my own feet, my weird not-quite-psychic instincts might provide a little more assistance on the sleuthing front.

Either way, I could only do my best. Yes, Archie was counting on me, but just knowing how much he appreciated my efforts made me feel a lot better about the situation.

Just as I had the day before, I went backstage with my little overnight bag and plastic-swathed ballgown, and changed out of my street clothes. To my infinite relief, this dress was much more comfortable, if not as elegant, telling me the afternoon wouldn't be quite the endurance contest that the day before had been.

I didn't recognize any of the women in the backstage area, probably because the final dance of the afternoon was country-western, and there wasn't a huge amount of overlap between those dancers and the ones who participated in the traditional and Latin competitions. From what I could tell, anyone who wanted to change into a ballgown had either already done so, or might have gotten dressed at home.

What I didn't know about country-western

dancing could have taken up an entire set of encyclopedias, but I had to admit it was fun to watch the competitors, a diversion that almost made me forget about the upcoming "all-in" dance and the awards ceremony to follow.

Of course, those moments of ease disappeared as soon as Eddie came up the bleacher steps toward the end of the two-step, sat down in the empty chair next to me, and murmured, "Ready for the final dance?"

"Sure," I replied, even though I didn't know for certain whether I was telling the truth or not. Yes, this last dance was just for show, but what if I stumbled so badly that the judges decided to go back to their tally sheets and recalculate Eddie's and my performance of the day before?

I told myself not to be ridiculous, that the judging at these things didn't work that way.

Or at least, I didn't think it did.

But with the country-western competition over, it was time for Eddie and me—and the rest of the novice and open amateur dancers—to make our way to the dance floor and take our positions. It was a lot more crowded than when we'd danced our routines the day before, because of course this dance included everyone, not just a single division.

My eyes scanned the crowd, spotting Joanna Greer in her signature bright lime green. She stood on the opposite side of the dance floor from where

Eddie and I waited for the music to begin, her expression almost impatient.

Was she, like me, just wanting all this to be over? True, her performance in the Latin had been spectacular, but she'd fumbled the traditional section enough that I doubted she would earn top prizes in both categories, and maybe she was looking forward to the chance to get the heck out of here and try again later when the stakes weren't so high.

I also saw Peter, who waited with his partner just a few couples away from where Joanna was standing. His partner was a pretty girl maybe in her early twenties, with sandy-blonde hair slicked back into a severe chignon. However, his attention wasn't on her, but on Joanna as she murmured something in an undertone to her companion.

Well, considering Joanna's acid-green dress and the amount of cleavage it displayed—she was wearing a ballgown, not a tango dress, but it still managed to be extremely revealing—I didn't think it too strange that Peter might have been staring at Joanna rather than his dance partner.

The music started then, the "Merry Widow," which I wasn't sure was the best choice of songs, considering what had happened to Brad Masters only a few weeks before. Yes, he and Joanna hadn't been married, but still.

However, I had to put my own thoughts on the

subject aside so I could concentrate on the dance. Despite my worries of a few minutes earlier, I didn't honestly think the judges would use my performance in this final waltz as a weapon, but on the other hand, I didn't want to do so badly that people might start wondering how I ever could have won a prize.

*If* I won one. It didn't matter that even Archie thought I'd danced well; I was probably the rankest of beginners at this competition, and there was a very strong chance that Eddie and I would go home empty-handed. If that happened, I knew it would be my fault, not his.

The "Merry Widow" moved on to the waltz from Swan Lake before we all glided to a stop as the music ended. Unlike the multi-dance elements of the tournament, we wouldn't be moving on to a foxtrot or a tango—the competition had opened with a waltz and was now concluding with one.

Because of where we'd ended up when the song closed, Eddie and I were standing about as far away from the podium as possible. Maybe a good thing... and a sign from the universe. If we really had made it to the top three, wouldn't we be closer so we wouldn't have to walk all that distance to collect our trophies?

The awards were handed out in reverse order of when the individual heats had been danced, so the country-western winners were called first, followed by the senior and the youth divisions.

Because I'd seen the way she and her partner had danced in the Latin competition, I wasn't too surprised to hear Joanna Greer's name called as the first place winner in the open amateur division. The couple didn't even place in the traditional, which again, I supposed was to have been expected.

However, her chin was up and her eyes narrow as the winners collected their trophies, telling me that, even if she wasn't totally surprised by the outcome, she also wasn't very happy about it. Was she wondering what would have happened if Brad Masters hadn't been taken from her so tragically and unexpectedly?

I didn't know, because, even though some people might have thought I had psychic powers, I definitely couldn't read minds. In fact, my talent for seeing auras—which had never been all that reliable—seemed to have deserted me entirely this weekend. It wasn't the first time I'd gone days without seeing one of those telltale glows around another person, giving me insight into what they were thinking and feeling, but for it to be AWOL when I really could have used it felt like a personal affront.

The judges moved on to announcing the winners in the novice category, and I felt myself tense, could practically sense the anticipation thrumming through every inch of Eddie's lean form. Even though it was true that he probably wouldn't have competed at all if Archie hadn't reached out and offered me as a replacement partner, I hated the thought of letting him down. He'd been an excellent dance partner, and also someone who'd done a lot to put me at ease by being completely relaxed about the whole situation, making it seem as though he'd be fine even if we didn't win a thing.

The third- and second-place winners were announced, and the little lump of anxiety in my stomach seemed to grow even heavier. If we hadn't won either of those titles, then there was absolutely no way—

"Novice division, traditional competition, first place...Edward Bixby and Selena Marx."

No way. It wasn't possible. I'd only been dancing for a few weeks. This had to be some kind of mistake.

"We won, Selena!" Eddie whispered urgently in my ear. "Come on—they're waiting for us."

Still feeling dazed, I let him grab me by the hand and drag me through the crowd and toward the podium. The faces of the other dancers passed by in a blur, which I supposed was a good thing. I had to think that some of my competitors in the novice division weren't too happy about having an upstart like me usurp the coveted first-place prize, and their expressions might have reflected that unfortunate fact.

"Congratulations," one of the judges, a slim, taut-looking woman in her forties, told me, then handed over a trophy.

*Not two?* I thought as I took it with shaking fingers, and then realized the trophies were awarded to couples, not individuals.

Well, that was fine. I'd let Eddie keep it. He was the one who'd really earned us that first-place win, while all I'd done was try to keep up and not make an utter fool of myself.

"And this," the judge added, handing an envelope to Eddie.

Right. We'd just won twenty-five thousand dollars.

Eddie could have that as well. I didn't need it, and again, he was the one who'd really earned the money, not me.

Still feeling as though I was walking through some sort of psychedelic haze, I followed him through the crowd and up to the risers where Calvin and Victoria were waiting for us. All along the way, people offered congratulations and shook Eddie's hand, although no one tried to hug me. Not that I minded being hugged, but since I didn't actually know any of those people, it would have been just a bit awkward.

However, the fierce embrace I got from Calvin

was definitely wanted, even if I was fighting off a massive attack of impostor syndrome. I couldn't have just won first place...could I?

"I always said you were amazing," my husband told me after he let me go.

I stared up at him, a bit breathless from the bear hug he'd just given me. "In this case, I think it was mostly Eddie's doing."

"You were both great," Victoria said. I could tell she was shocked by this turn of events, if impressed and happy for both me and for Eddie. "And I can't wait to tell Archie. He's going to be thrilled!"

Yes, he probably would be, although I couldn't help thinking he'd be even happier if I'd come out of this tournament with some solid leads, rather than a trophy and a check I had no intention of cashing.

Or two checks, actually—Eddie opened the envelope and extracted a cashier's check with my name on it and filled out for exactly twelve thousand, five hundred dollars. Even as he tried to hand it to me, I shook my head.

"That should be yours," I told him, and he sent me a puzzled look.

"We both won," he said.

"I couldn't have won without you as my partner," I responded. "And I want you to have it. Let me sign it over to you."

He blinked, then looked at Calvin, as if he wasn't sure whether my husband might bring up some objections to his wife handing over such a big chunk of money.

But Calvin knew better than to protest. We had a household account, into which we both deposited enough funds to keep everything running smoothly, but he'd never once asked to have access to the enormous amounts I had in my various checking, savings, and investment accounts. He'd told me on more than one occasion that the money had been mine before we got married, so he didn't have any right to it.

I didn't entirely agree with his view of the situation, but I also knew arguing with him about it wouldn't change things. And that was why I knew he would never tell me what I should do with the prize money I'd just won.

Still looking dubious, Eddie said, "It doesn't feel right."

Victoria sent him an amused look. "It's fine, Eddie. Selena's an independently wealthy woman."

"You are?" he blurted out, after giving a startled blink.

"Yes," I said. It was common enough knowledge around Globe that I was sitting on a pretty big pile of cash, so it felt almost strange to realize Eddie had absolutely no idea that handing over twelve and a half grand wasn't going to hurt my finances even the littlest bit. "Here."

My friend had obviously been expecting my next move, because she extracted a pen from her purse and handed both the pen and her bag to me, presumably so I'd have a semi-solid surface to write on, since tables and desks were kind of in short supply in the auditorium. I carefully wrote my name on the back of the check and then gave it to Eddie before slipping the pen into Victoria's purse and handing it back to her.

"There," I said, and grinned up into Eddie's still dumbfounded face. "Anyone want to get a celebratory drink?"

## 10

## Sick Burn

THAT SINGLE CELEBRATORY DRINK TURNED into two, along with a round of appetizers. But a little before six, Calvin and Victoria and I drove back to Globe. Victoria had already texted Archie to tell him the good news, and he'd offered to take us all out to dinner at the Gold Dust casino's restaurant, since nothing else was open in town on a Sunday evening...unless we wanted to hit the local Dairy Queen, that is.

But the occasion seemed to call for something a little more special than burgers and shakes, so we'd all agreed to the plan. Before we left the resort, I'd changed back into my regular clothes, although there wasn't much I could do about my overdone makeup and competition-appropriate chignon.

*Well, it never hurts to shake things up a little bit,* I thought with an inner grin. Even though it didn't seem as if I had much to show for my undercover efforts this weekend—well, except a trophy and a *very* happy Eddie Bixby—I told myself I could put aside my worry over Archie's plight for a couple of hours. Obviously, he wasn't horribly disappointed in me, or he wouldn't have suggested dinner.

He met us at the restaurant, looking dapper in a sport jacket over a deep peacock-blue shirt. Most of the time, I wouldn't have thought the casino's restaurant required such fancy duds, since a lot of its patrons were tourists passing through, but because Calvin and Victoria were already dressed up, and my change of clothes had been a pretty sundress because the day was so hot, we all looked like we matched pretty well.

"First place!" he exclaimed when we met in the restaurant's waiting area next to the hostess station, then gave me a very uncharacteristic hug. "I'm so proud of you!"

"Well, it was mostly your instruction," I told him. "And having Eddie as a partner."

Victoria just shook her head. "And you, too, Selena. You shouldn't sell yourself short."

"She's right," Calvin put in. "I'm pretty sure Archie could give me five years of lessons, and I still wouldn't be able to pull off what you just did."

"Oh, I think I could do it in three," Archie quipped. He was smiling, but his bright expression suddenly faded...and I thought I knew why.

If I couldn't find out who really had killed Brad Masters, then Archie wouldn't be around to teach Calvin...or anyone else...how to do the foxtrot.

The hostess, a cousin of Calvin's named Janelle, came up to us, menus in hand, so we abandoned the subject as she led us over to a booth in a corner. Because it was a Sunday night, the place wasn't very crowded, probably the reason why we'd gotten some prime seats at such late notice.

Then again, the casino and restaurant were owned by the San Ramon Apache tribe, and Calvin was their police chief. He and I got a good table pretty much every time we went to the restaurant, so I had a feeling his status with the tribe might also have had something to do with it.

We'd all been there so many times that none of us really had to look at the menu, although there was some lively discussion as to which kind of wine we should order. Once that was taken care of and our server had come back with the bottle and poured some for all of us, Archie lifted his glass.

"To Selena," he said. "A woman full of surprises."

I supposed I had surprised him—and myself—so I smiled as I raised my glass. "And to all of you for supporting me and my crazy plans."

We drank, but when he set down his glass, Archie looked deadly serious again. "So...did you learn anything useful?"

"Not really," I said, feeling my own moment of excitement deflate like a balloon that had just been poked with a pin. "But you know how it goes. Sometimes it takes a while for things to percolate. I'm sure I actually did pick up some tidbits that could help in the long run, but for now, I'm just going to have to wait and see if any of them end up making sense."

His lips might have thinned a little bit, but Archie had known me long enough to realize I worked through flashes of inspiration and not slow, methodical deductive reasoning, so giving me grief over coming home empty-handed regarding the murder investigation wasn't going to help the situation any.

Calvin chimed in, saying, "Selena has a great track record with this kind of thing. We just have to be patient."

Victoria and Archie exchanged a glance. Neither of them said anything, but they didn't have to. Their wedding date had been set for October fourteenth, which should have given us plenty of time to get this whole mess straightened out. However, since it was now the middle of June and I still didn't have a single clue to go on, I feared those next four months were going to slip by uncomfortably fast.

However, Victoria managed to summon a smile, then said, "This will be a great success story for your studio, Archie. I know people are going to want to take lessons from you once they hear how Selena danced her way to first place after only a few weeks of practice."

Her comment got us past that awkward moment, as I was sure she'd hoped it would. All during the meal, though, I could only think of one thing.

I had to fix this. I just had to.

Going to work at the shop the next morning felt like something of an anticlimax, although I told myself I had a case of the Mondays and nothing else. Archie, on the other hand, seemed a lot perkier than I'd expected him to be.

"Did you see this?" he asked, and handed his phone over to me. For someone who'd only entered twenty-first-century life a year earlier, he had adapted remarkably well to its technology.

On his phone's screen was an article from the Arizona *Sun*. I hadn't even looked at the news that morning, since I'd been running late and didn't have much time to waste. I stared down at Archie's phone, my eyes quickly scanning the article. It appeared the medical examiner's office had released their full report on Brad Masters' death, reaffirming that he'd died from that single stab wound to the chest. The interesting thing, though, was that all his wounds had been cauterized, which explained why Victoria hadn't seen a godawful mess when she opened the steamer trunk and found Brad's body inside.

"'Cauterized'?" I repeated as I handed the phone back to Archie.

He gave me a nod that was almost triumphant. "That's what the coroner said. I have absolutely no idea how you would even go about doing such a thing, which is yet another reason why Detective Murphy's case against me is so weak."

Honestly, I didn't know how to cauterize a wound, either. I vaguely recalled a few grisly scenes from movies where people had to perform the procedure using a hot log from a fire or something equally implausible, but I doubted that was the means the killer had used to make sure Brad hadn't left a trail of blood from the spot where the murder —and the butchery—had taken place to the back-stage area where Archie's steamer trunk waited.

"Do you think it's enough to make them drop the case?" I asked, and Archie's triumphant expression slipped a little.

"I don't know," he replied. "I contacted my attorney as soon as I saw the article, and he said that, while it should help build my defense, he doubted it would get the D.A. to back off. Right now, I'm the only suspect, and the optics wouldn't be very good if the police ended up letting me go without having someone else in custody."

No, I supposed it wouldn't. I hated how these sorts of things could get so political, but I'd been on this planet long enough to understand that was how such situations often played out.

"Well, it's still good news," I assured my friend, and he nodded…although not as enthusiastically as he might have a few minutes earlier.

"Yes. Even if this thing goes to trial, the jury will see that this is the sort of murder I couldn't possibly have committed."

While I agreed with the sentiment, the phrasing left a little to be desired. "What, Archie…does that mean there are some kinds of murder you *might* commit?"

At once, his hands planted on the hips of his perfectly pressed khakis. I knew he owned at least a couple of pairs of jeans, because I'd seen him wear them on the weekend from time to time, but he never showed up for work in anything less formal than slacks and a button-down shirt with a sweater in the winter, and khakis and polo shirts in the summer.

"There are some mice who might have met the wrong end of my paw over the years," he said crisply, confirming a suspicion I'd already been harboring for a while.

His comment brought up another topic I'd

been loath to broach, even though I knew I couldn't let it go any longer.

"Archie," I said quietly, "you really need to tell her."

Instead of responding, he glanced toward the street. A couple of kids who looked as though they might be high school juniors or seniors walked past the big picture window at the front of the store, but clearly, they were intent on some other destination, since they didn't even spare a glance at the shop...or at the two of us, standing near a table with a display of books and crystals focused on the summer solstice and summer energy in general.

At least Archie didn't try to fend me off by asking precisely what it was he needed to tell Victoria. No, his lips pressed together and he looked less than happy with me, but after another pause, he said, "How am I supposed to do that? She's going to think I'm crazy."

"She won't," I replied firmly. "Because I'll back you up. I'll tell her how I found you on my balcony two years ago, and how you stayed with me until you were able to break the curse. Calvin can corroborate the story, too."

Once again, Archie went silent for a moment. I knew he hadn't been overly happy about concealing the truth of his origins from his fiancée, but had kept quiet because he feared her reaction to the news.

When he spoke again, his voice was barely more than a murmur. "What if she leaves me?"

"I can't see Victoria doing that," I said. And it was true; she was a very practical, down-to-earth sort of person, but she'd had enough exposure to my mystical practices over the past year that she was beginning to understand there was more to this world than merely what we could experience with our five senses. "She loves you, Archie. She'll understand. But you have to tell her. Do you really want to start a life together with such a big secret standing between you?"

He shoved his hands in his pockets, breaking the smooth line of his expertly tailored khakis. Merely doing such a thing told me how harrowed up his mind must be, because normally, Archie took great care with his clothing.

"Of course I don't," he said, now sounding exasperated. "But if the D.A. has his way, I won't have a life with her. I won't have any kind of life at all. Do you really think it's such a good idea to bring up this whole mess about being a cat if there's a very good chance I'm going to be behind bars for the rest of my life?"

The anguish in his expression made me go over and put a hand on his arm so I could give it a reassuring squeeze. "That's not going to happen," I told him. "I won't let it."

For a second, he looked down at me, his mouth

tight. "Then you'd better hope your intuition kicks in very soon."

And he pulled his arm from my grasp and went over to the bookshelves, then pretended to busy himself with putting the volumes there back in order.

I briefly contemplated going over to him and really having it out—after all, it didn't look as if we were going to be interrupted by a bunch of customers any time soon—but then decided I'd better let it go. After all, I knew what it was like to be suspected of murder, although in my case, I'd been going up against Calvin, not some faceless D.A. who only cared about his conviction record.

Despite all that, I really wished Archie would tell Victoria the truth. She deserved to know. Also, even if he wouldn't admit it to himself, I knew he would feel awful if he was convicted of this murder and sent to prison with such a big lie hanging between them.

For the briefest moment, I wondered whether I should go to her and share what I knew about Archie's history, but almost immediately, I shoved the thought away. This was his story to tell, and besides, I realized he would never forgive me for meddling like that. I cared about Victoria and considered her one of my closest friends, and yet I also knew that Archie came first in my heart. He was the one I'd rescued from my balcony all those months ago, the one who'd become the brother I'd never had.

No, if he was determined to keep this secret, there wasn't much I could do about it.

———

The two of us were stiff and formal with one another the rest of that day, and I was much more relieved than I wanted to admit when five o'clock finally rolled around and I could put my little "be back at" sign in the window. Not that people probably cared too much, since we'd had a grand total of five customers that day, but I knew I'd go in to work even if no one showed up to shop.

For just a minute, I wondered if the lack of customers had anything to do with Archie's current uncertain legal status, but I pushed the thought away. We'd had plenty of people coming and going the two weeks after his arrest, so I didn't think that was the problem. No, this was just the summer doldrums, when people had better things to do than spend time indoors. Also, Mondays generally stank for sales unless they were close to the holidays. I had to believe things would get better as the week wore on.

Or at least, the shopping part of the week promised to improve. I had no idea whether I should be as hopeful about the state of Archie's and my relationship.

Calvin had worked the six-to-three shift that day, so he was already there when I got back to the house. Sadie danced around me, tail wagging with glee, and I bent down to pat her on the head even as my husband came out of the kitchen to give me a hug.

"I thought I'd barbecue some chicken skewers tonight," he said, then paused after taking a good look at my face. "Something wrong?"

"Oh, Archie and I disagreed over whether he should tell Victoria the truth about who he is and where he came from," I replied, then let out a sigh. "I know I shouldn't butt in, but I also don't think it's fair to Victoria."

My husband almost always wore his long black hair in a tight ponytail, so he couldn't run a hand through it without making an unholy mess. He had to settle for rubbing his chin, and said, "That's a rough one. But it's probably good that you stay out of it."

Well, at least my husband agreed this was not a good time for me to be a busybody. "What happens if she does find out someday?" I asked next. "Won't she be angry with us for not saying anything to her?"

"Maybe," Calvin allowed, then twined his fingers with mine. "But I still think this is between the two of them. And I also think I should pour you a glass of wine."

Oh, how I loved that man of mine. "Wine would be awesome," I said.

The two of us went into the kitchen, where he got an already open bottle of sauvignon blanc out of the fridge and then fetched some stemless wine glasses from the cupboard. He filled the bottom inch or so of my glass and did the same with his.

Next came the customary clink of our wine glasses together, although neither of us offered a toast. Frankly, right then I didn't think we had a whole heck of a lot to celebrate, my victory at the competition over the weekend notwithstanding.

Instead, I told Calvin about what the medical examiner's report had said about all of Brad Masters' wounds being cauterized, a recitation that got me a knowing nod.

"That explains a lot," my husband said. "I kept wondering why there wasn't more physical evidence in the backstage area."

A nicely delicate way of describing what should have been a trail of blood and gore.

"Do you know what would cauterize a wound like that?" I asked next. After all, my husband was the one with a degree in criminology, not me.

He took a contemplative sip of sauv blanc, frowning slightly. "Well, the most common way to cauterize a wound is to do it chemically, with silver nitrate. But you're saying the M.E.'s report indicates Brad Masters' wounds were cauterized by burning?"

"That's what I read," I replied. "They didn't go into a huge amount of detail, though."

"Well, if his wounds really were burned, then pretty much anything that was hot enough should do the trick," Calvin said. "A heated blade, a branding iron...."

"Good thing Chuck wasn't anywhere around," I quipped, and Calvin gave me a sideways look that was half pained, half amused.

To be honest, I didn't even know whether our friend Chuck used branding irons on his livestock, but since he was the only person in my acquaintance who actually raised cattle, by necessity I'd had to use his name in my little joke.

"Anyway," Calvin went on, obviously deciding he wasn't going to directly respond to my remark, "the point is, a lot of different things could have been used, especially since the killer was working on a dead body and wouldn't have had to worry about introducing any toxins or foreign agents the same way you might if you were just trying to do some emergency first aid by cauterizing a wound."

I hadn't even thought of that particular angle, but I supposed it made sense. A lot of concerns kind of flew out the window when your patient was already dead.

"So...this isn't the sort of thing someone would do on a whim," I said slowly, and Calvin gave a grim little laugh.

"Not at all. The initial stabbing, sure. But cutting the guy up, making sure his wounds wouldn't continue to bleed, hiding him in Archie's steamer trunk...." The words trailed off, and my husband's mouth twisted before he lifted the glass of wine to his lips and took what looked to me like a much-needed swallow. "No, this was planned. Someone thought a long time about how to kill Brad Masters and the best way to handle the crime so no one would be thinking of him as a suspect." Another pause, and Calvin added, looking almost amused, "At least, I have a feeling the killer was a man. But I suppose I shouldn't be making assumptions like that."

Maybe not—Calvin was always about being fair, not too surprising in a full-on Libra—and yet I also had every instinct telling me this wasn't something a woman would have done.

I thought then of the Magician card I'd pulled when I was first trying to get a read on the crime, on what could have possibly motivated such a horrible act of violence. The whole thing seemed way too premeditated to be a crime of passion, which made me wonder what else could have caused Brad Masters to be targeted in such a way.

Money? I knew next to nothing about the

man, but his bio had been in the program for everyone to see—the same program that called me a "small business owner" while neglecting to mention that the business in question was a New Age shop, and that I was a practicing witch.

No big deal, I supposed. A lot of people still had issues with those of us who practiced alternate forms of spirituality, so the event's organizers had probably decided it was better to gloss over any elements in my background that might give some pause. Anyway, there hadn't been anything in Brad's bio that would have merited a second look. He owned an insurance agency in Tempe and was unmarried, and had been competing in ballroom dance tournaments for more than ten years. Maybe an insurance agency was worth a lot of money, but I kind of doubted it...or that his business had been the reason for the murder.

There was definitely something else going on here. What, I didn't know, because the more I wracked my brains, going over everything that had happened at the competition and trying to come up with even one small detail, one odd intonation or comment that might lead me to the perpetrator, the more I realized I didn't have a single thing to go on.

I summoned a wan smile. "Well, if you definitely think the killer is a man, I suppose that narrows it down just a little."

Calvin responded to my smile with one of his own, although I had a feeling his looked a lot more genuine. "Just a little. But come on—we're not going to solve this thing right now, and we might as well go out in the sunshine and get those skewers on the grill."

That sounded like a great idea to me. When I worked until five and he didn't, Calvin did his best to handle the cooking, which in the summer meant a lot of barbecue. And that was good, because I could sit in the sun with my glass of wine and soak in its welcome warmth, and do my best to put the conundrum of Brad Masters' murder out of my brain, if even for a little while.

Unfortunately, I knew this particular problem wasn't going anywhere anytime soon.

## 11

## Double Jeopardy

THE NEXT DAY, AN UNNATURALLY cheerful Archie greeted me as I came into the shop about fifteen minutes before opening.

"Good morning!" he called out, and I blinked. No, he wasn't the sort of person who was a grumpy Gus even after consuming several cups of coffee, but considering the way we'd parted the day before...and especially when you looked at everything that was currently going on in his life...I definitely hadn't expected to have him address me quite so happily this morning. It wasn't quite as strange that he'd gotten to work before me, since he had his own set of keys and used to beat me in all the time when he was living in the apartment over the store. However, now that he and Victoria had bought Miriam Jacobsen's former house and moved in together, he usually wasn't quite as eager to be the first one at the shop.

"Um...good morning," I replied. "How're you today?"

"Great," Archie responded, still looking way too happy for a man out on bail for a murder he didn't commit. "I thought about what you said, so I talked to Victoria last night."

About all I could do was blink at him. Judging by his demeanor this morning, I had to think the discussion had gone well, but....

"And...?" I asked.

He went over to the cash register and unlocked it, then started matter-of-factly placing small bills and coins in the various compartments. We hardly ever did any cash transactions these days, but it somehow felt wrong not to have the register stocked, and Archie had always been the kind of person who found comfort in following routines.

Once he was done, he looked up, a small smile still touching his lips. "And she was a little disbelieving at first—which I'd expected—but as I started to fill in the details, to tell her things no one who hadn't been alive back then could have possibly known, she realized I was telling the truth."

"And she wasn't freaked out?"

Now he almost grinned. "Victoria isn't the kind of person who generally 'freaks out.' No, she was quiet for a moment or two, and then she told me that she loved me for me, and it didn't matter where I'd come from or what might have happened to me in the past. In fact, she said it made a lot of sense, considering that the story about me being your cousin had never felt right to her, for whatever reason." A pause, and he added, looking sly, "She said she'd wondered if I was an old boyfriend of yours or something, and the two of us just didn't want to tell her the truth."

"Goddess, no," I said in tones of convincing horror. Archie and me as a couple? Never in a million years. "I'm glad you were able to disabuse her of that notion."

He grinned. "Well, my history as a talking cat did clear things up on that front."

Yes, I supposed it might have. And I was extremely glad to know Victoria had taken the news in stride. I had to wonder whether I would have done the same in a similar situation, and reassured myself that I'd been dealing with the strange and unusual for much of my adult life, so a fiancé who'd spent a good chunk of his very long existence as an alley cat shouldn't have been that big a deal.

After all, my own husband was a coyote shapeshifter, and that particular bit of knowledge hadn't kept me from wanting to be with him. I'd only seen him shift that one time at the very beginning of our acquaintance, well before we were even together; the people in his tribe were careful to hide that part of themselves from outsiders, and although I couldn't exactly be viewed as an outsider anymore, Calvin still seemed reticent to reveal that side of his nature.

But there had been a few times when I'd woken up in the middle of the night to find myself alone in our bedroom, and then heard the far-off cry of a coyote and realized he'd slipped away to reacquaint himself with his animal side. He never stayed away very long, and it didn't seem to matter whether there was a full moon or not. The San Ramon Apache weren't werewolves, weren't controlled by the phases of the moon. No, they only shifted into their coyote form when they felt they were getting too distant from their animal natures and needed to renew that connection.

Anyway, because my own husband wasn't exactly what you could call a run-of-the-mill guy, I had to believe I would have dealt with Archie's revelations just fine.

That Victoria had also been able to do so just made me love her that much more.

The week slipped past quietly enough, and although Josie popped in several times wanting to know more about the murder case, I really didn't have much to tell her.

"You haven't come up with anything?" she asked, looking disappointed.

Because she and Archie weren't exactly besties, I didn't know whether her disappointment stemmed from worry on his behalf, or dissatisfaction that my hedgewitch gifts didn't seem to be up to snuff this particular go-'round. While I couldn't help agreeing with that sentiment, I also knew I couldn't sugarcoat the situation.

"Not really," I replied. I'd tried several more Tarot pulls and had only come up with what I liked to call minor-arcana mishmash, meaning the cards didn't look as though they intended to provide me with anything more than what they already had. The image of the Magician card from the original pull didn't seem to want to leave my brain, although I really had no idea why it was so important. The card didn't fit anything I knew about Brad Masters, and neither did it seem to apply to anyone important in his life. It wasn't as though Joanna Greer moonlit as a magician's assistant or something. No, the brief bio I'd read about her said she was a licensed cosmetologist and aesthetician, and worked in a spa in Scottsdale.

Well, either the meaning of the Magician card would reveal itself eventually, or it wouldn't. Just the day before, Archie had told me the trial had been scheduled for the end of August, which felt like it should have been enough time for things to work themselves out but which I worried would be gone before I knew it.

Josie's auburn-penciled brows pulled together. It was a scorchingly hot day, with temperatures already well past ninety even though it wasn't yet noon, but she still wore a linen jacket over her sleeveless blouse. Despite the heat, she never seemed to break a sweat, and I wondered what her secret was.

Pure unflappable nerves, probably.

I also wondered how she'd known the exact right time to drop in when Archie wouldn't be in the store. He had a meeting with his lawyer in Mesa, and I'd gone ahead and given him the day off, thinking he probably wouldn't want to come back to work after doing something that had to be emotionally draining. Since Wednesdays tended to be extremely quiet, I knew I'd be able to get along fine without him here, even as I worried about what his attorney might be telling him.

"But it's been three weeks," she pointed out, a sad fact of which I was all too aware. In the past, I'd often been able to get to the bottom of a murder in ten days or less, but it didn't seem as though I was going to be quite so lucky this time around.

"I know," I said. "But the trial isn't until the end of August."

Josie perked up immediately at that news, telling me I'd offered her a tidbit she hadn't yet been privy to. While the story hadn't died down completely, the lack of any new developments meant it had been pushed back behind that day's latest car crashes or house fires or whatever story the local newscasts had deemed much more interesting and more likely to draw in viewers. At least, I hadn't seen any mention of the trial date being set, and I'd set up a Google alert so I'd know when the story popped up again.

"Oh," Josie replied, "then you have lots of time."

Something I'd also tried to tell myself, although I kept getting the uncomfortable feeling that I didn't have as much time as I might think. Victoria and Archie had steadfastly gone ahead with their wedding planning, mostly because the event would be a small one held in the backyard of their new home, and therefore they wouldn't have to worry about cancellation fees from a rented venue. There were still the flowers and the catering and the rest of it to worry about, but Victoria had told me they could cancel as late as mid-September and only lose a ten-percent fee.

Yes, by mid-September, we should definitely know Archie's fate...one way or another.

"Maybe," I allowed. "But I don't want this thing hanging over Archie's and Victoria's heads any longer than it has to. They should be having fun planning their wedding, not worrying about whether he's going to end up in prison."

Josie responded with a sympathetic nod. While she wasn't a huge fan of Archie, she positively adored Victoria and didn't want to see anything bad happen to her...or the man she loved. "It does sound like it's going to be a lovely wedding."

I thought so, too. Obviously, Archie didn't have any family who would attend—his parents had passed away while he was trapped in a cat's body, and he'd been an only child, and therefore didn't have any nieces or nephews or their offspring who might still be around. He probably still had some first cousins two or three times removed out there somewhere, but since he didn't know any of them, there wouldn't be much point in inviting them to the wedding. And while Victoria did have siblings, they all had young children and lived in Michigan, and traveling all the way to Arizona would have been too much trouble. Only her parents would be attending, along with some friends Victoria and Archie had made in Globe and a few of Victoria's sorority sisters from ASU, meaning the affair would be a much smaller one than Calvin's and my wedding, which had hundreds of people there to celebrate our union.

"It will be," I said. "And the house is looking

gorgeous. Victoria has really made the place look new all over again."

"She's a very talented designer," Josie observed. "And a wonderful wedding planner. So I know it will be perfect."

"If it happens," I replied gloomily, and Josie reached over and patted my hand.

"You'll work it out, Selena," she said. "You always do."

Her phone binged from within her oversized purse, signaling a new text had come in, and she pulled out her shiny red iPhone and frowned down at the screen.

"I have to go," she told me. "One of my clients needs to move up her one o'clock meeting with me. But you take care."

After offering me an encouraging smile, Josie sailed out of the shop, cell phone already pressed to her ear.

I watched her leave, and desperately hoped she was right about how I'd work it out. At the moment, I felt as though I was floundering in a mud pit, with no one to come along and throw me a rope.

All I could do was hope I'd be able to reach out and grab a lifeline sooner rather than later.

194 • CHRISTINE POPE

Later that day, Victoria came in, looking so glowing and happy, I wondered if the D.A. had suddenly decided to drop the charges against Archie.

When I asked her, however, her expression fell for a moment before she perked back up again.

"If only," she said. "I talked to Archie, and he told me the lawyer was encouraging but that not much had really changed. We're sort of in a holding pattern."

I knew the feeling.

"But I got some other great news," she continued. "You know that new neighborhood they're building to the east of town, Mariposa Heights?"

I nodded. The development had broken ground a few months ago, promising a hundred new homes on large plots of land. Personally, I didn't know whether there was enough demand in little Globe to support such a project—and I knew Josie hated the thought of competing with the prospect of brand-new houses when her portfolio consisted entirely of representing people selling older homes—but other than that, I didn't know a lot about it.

"Well," Victoria said, "the developer reached out to me and said he was interested in hiring me to stage the model homes! It would be wonderful to have a project like that in my portfolio, something that will show other developers I can do large-scale projects and not just individual houses."

It did sound like a great opportunity for my friend, no matter what my personal feelings about the development might be. "That's wonderful," I told her.

She nodded. "I should know whether they're going to hire me by the end of next week. However, the project also got me thinking. I've been working from my home office all this time because I figured I shouldn't invest in office space until I know my design business is bringing in enough to support it. But if this deal goes through, I'll definitely have the capital to start working outside the house, maybe even hire office help. I thought maybe you'd have an idea about what was available here, since you work downtown."

Honestly, it was the sort of thing she probably should have asked Josie. But since Victoria was no dummy, she'd probably also realized—after watching Josie and Archie interact during the purchase of Miriam Jacobsen's former home—that involving Josie in another real estate transaction wasn't the best idea.

And then it came to me.

"Why not the apartment?" I asked, pointing upward at the flat that had been my home for my first year and a half here in Globe. It had been sitting empty ever since Archie and Victoria moved in together, mostly because I couldn't think of what to do with it. I definitely didn't want to sell the apartment, and I also didn't want to use it as an Airbnb. While it was no longer my home, I still had fond memories of the place and wanted to take care of it as best I could.

But having Victoria take it over and turn it into her studio sounded like the perfect solution. It would need some remodeling, obviously, but it was around 1,700 square feet, definitely large enough to accommodate a design studio and an office, maybe even a reception space.

I told her as much, and she frowned.

"I thought you wanted to hang on to your apartment," she said, and I smiled.

"Yes, I thought I did," I replied. "But now something's telling me it's time to let it go. And I can't think of anyone who deserves it more."

She paused for a moment, finely arched brows drawing together as she seemed to contemplate my offer. Because she'd been in my apartment when she was helping me plan my wedding to Calvin, she knew the general layout of the space, and was probably better equipped than I was to decide whether it would work for her needs or not.

"I'll need to knock down a few walls," she warned me, and I shrugged.

"I figured you would. But can you try to keep the exposed brick on the wall with fireplace?"

"Oh, I'd never get rid of that," she assured me. "It's gorgeous, and adds so much character to the space. But we'll need to do something about access —remodel the stairs and the entrance off the parking lot, possibly make a little lobby, or...." She stopped there and sent me a sheepish look. "Maybe I'm getting ahead of myself."

"No, that all sounds great," I said. "I really like the idea of remodeling the back entrance so people could either go up the stairs to your studio or come into my shop on the ground floor. It means I'll have dual access from both the parking lot and the street, which might help to bring in more traffic."

She didn't respond for a moment, her expression now distracted, as if she'd already started moving walls and choosing flooring in her mind. Then she asked, "How much do you want for it?"

"Nothing," I said immediately, and her eyes widened. Yes, pretty much everyone in Globe knew I'd been generous in donating to local charities and doing what I could to make the town a better place, but I could tell she hadn't been expecting an offer like this. I added, "The apartment is just sitting there, doing nothing. I'd love for you to take it over."

"Oh, I couldn't take it for free—" she began.

"Then I'll charge you a dollar for it," I cut in, smiling. "And if you need any help with the remodeling costs, just let me know."

"No, I'll take care of that part of the project," Victoria replied, her tone firm enough I knew she wasn't going to allow me to argue that particular point. "I've got the funds for that as long as I don't go too crazy. But I'll know for sure after I have a contractor come and look at the place, just because it's an old building, and they're generally full of surprises."

I wouldn't know about that, since the apartment and the store beneath had both been completely updated and renovated when I moved in, and any nightmares of old wiring or rotted joists had been well in the past. Still, it sounded as though she was going to be taking down some walls...and probably removing the kitchen entirely, since I didn't think she would need it...and that meant she might be getting into places that hadn't been touched previously.

"Sounds like you have some phone calls to make," I said, and she smiled, now lit up by even more possibilities.

"I do," she said, then reached over and squeezed my hand. "Thank you, Selena. I mean it."

"Happy to help," I told her, and she nodded before telling me goodbye. She hurried out, clearly ready to get back to her home office so she could start contacting contractors and getting bids on the project.

And even though I knew I was probably letting myself in for some remodeling dust and general chaos over the next few months, I knew it would be worth it. Victoria would have the design studio of her dreams, and I wouldn't have to feel guilty about the way my poor apartment was being neglected.

If only I could solve Brad Masters' murder as easily.

## 12

## Partner Swap

I'd been a little apprehensive that Calvin might be annoyed with the impulsive way I'd handed over the apartment to Victoria without consulting him—even though it was my separate property, since I'd bought it before we were married—but he actually only nodded and said, "Sounds like a good idea."

We were sitting inside to have dinner that night because it was just too darn hot to be out on the patio. The house, with its thick adobe walls, stayed naturally cool most of the time, and for those days when even its sturdy construction wasn't enough to keep out the heat, Calvin had installed mini-split A/C units. One of them hummed away in the background, gamely doing its job of preventing us from expiring of heat prostration.

"You're not mad I didn't talk to you about it?" I asked.

He set down his glass of chardonnay. Because it was so warm, I'd made my famous Asian chicken salad for dinner, and the cool white wine went perfectly with it. "Of course not," he said. "That property is yours. You owned it before we even got together."

"You owned this house before we were married, but you put me on the deed," I pointed out.

"That's different," he replied at once. "This is your home now, too. I wanted to make sure you were on the deed in case anything ever happened to me."

A little shiver ran down my back, one that didn't have much to do with the air conditioning unit blowing cool air into the room from a few feet away. True, the majority of the time, Calvin's job didn't seem too dangerous, as most of his duties appeared to involve managing his deputies and occasionally rescuing a wayward cow from a field where it didn't belong, but I also understood I couldn't get too complacent about the situation. He'd also had to break up meth labs and intervene in domestic disputes, and the potential for confrontations like that going wrong was a lot higher than I really wanted to contemplate.

"Still," I said. "It was impulsive. I guess I was

feeling bad for Victoria and Archie, and wanted to do something nice for her."

Calvin smiled, and reached over so he could lay a reassuring hand on mine. "I'm kind of used to the whole 'impulsive' thing by now."

His comment lightened the mood a little, and I couldn't help grinning back at him. Unfortunately, the next words out of his mouth brought me right back down to earth.

"Besides," he went on, "it's probably a good idea to make sure Victoria is set up in her own career and doing well, just in case."

"'Just in case' what?" I shot back, even though I knew darn well what he was driving at.

"In case things don't go well at Archie's trial," Calvin said quietly. "I know it's something we don't want to think about, but we have to prepare ourselves for that possibility."

"You don't think I can solve the case?"

His dark eyes met mine, calm, filled with a sort of terrible understanding. "That's not what I said. You have a great track record, Selena. At the same time, though, it doesn't seem as if you have very many leads this go-'round."

There was the understatement of the year. Time and time again, I'd replayed everything I'd seen and heard at the Stepping Stars competition, and over and over again, I couldn't think of a single detail or conversation that had made me suspect any of the people I'd met there, not even the obviously slimy Ron Williams. For all I knew, the killer wasn't a member of the ballroom dance community at all, and had only disposed of Brad Master's body backstage at the tournament in an attempt to throw the police completely off the scent.

Well, if that was the scenario we were currently dealing with, then the culprit had definitely succeeded in achieving his goal.

"I know," I said. "I suppose I'm hoping that, even if this thing does go to trial, the jury is going to realize how sketchy the evidence is, how there really isn't much of a motive, and will go ahead and acquit him. But even if that happens, there are going to be some people who'll always believe Archie did it. I don't want a cloud of suspicion hanging over his head for the rest of his life. I want him to be completely exonerated."

Calvin's fingers tightened on mine. "I understand," he said. "And I know you're going to do everything you can to keep him from going to prison. All I'm saying is that I'm glad Victoria will be okay, no matter what happens in the end."

To be honest, I really didn't know if she would be okay. I'd been in the same dark place where I feared that the man I loved would be put behind bars for the rest of his life over something he hadn't even done, and trust me, it wasn't a good spot to be in. Calvin had been exonerated and Dillon James' real murderer was now rotting in a maximum-security prison, but there had been agonizing hours and days when I hadn't known that would be the eventual outcome of the case.

If all our worst fears came true and Archie was found guilty of Brad Masters' murder, how could Victoria ever be "okay"?

But I didn't try to argue with Calvin's statement. On the surface, maybe Victoria would be all right. She'd have a way to support herself, would have a supportive community here in Globe to be there for her when she needed us. If nothing else, that made me very glad she'd relocated from Scottsdale. From the way she'd talked about her life there, she'd been so busy that she really didn't have many friends or anyone she could rely on to help her out when she needed a shoulder to lean on. Whereas here, she had Calvin and me and Josie and Hazel and Chuck and many others who'd become a part of her circle.

That had to count for something.

I just had to make sure she wouldn't end up having to need all of us.

When he came to work the next day, Archie sent me a very direct look as he walked into the shop.

"You gave Victoria the apartment," he said, his tone flat.

For a second, I just stared back at him. Although his expression was neutral enough, I could tell from the way he'd made the statement that he wasn't very happy about the situation.

And that was something I hadn't been expecting. I'd feared that Calvin might not be completely thrilled with me, just because I'd given away a valuable piece of property without consulting him first. But I hadn't realized doing so might have incurred Archie's ire instead.

"I did," I said lightly. "She needed a place for her design studio, and right now the apartment is just wasted space." I stopped there for a moment, wondering whether I should say anything else. But I figured I might as well face this head on rather than trying to pretend nothing was wrong. "Is that a problem?"

His jaw hardened almost imperceptibly. "Did you give it to her because you're worried I might end up in prison?"

"No," I answered at once. While Calvin had jumped to that same conclusion, the idea had honestly never entered my mind until he brought it up. "I thought the space would be perfect for her, that's all. And I also think it would be fun to have her working upstairs, especially after you get your dance studio going and aren't here at the shop anymore."

It seemed Archie hadn't been expecting to hear those reasons as my motivation, because now he looked almost taken aback. "That's really why you gave the apartment to her?"

"Yes, it is," I said. "I understand why you might have thought differently, but it's not the case at all. You and Victoria are like family to me, and families look out for each other, right?"

"'Family,'" he repeated, his gaze meeting mine. In his face, I could see the strain of the past few weeks, but also a kind of relief, a realization that I was being completely honest with him about this.

I nodded. "We can choose our families, you know. I love my mother and Tom, but you know you're like the brother I never had, and I love Victoria because she's awesome and you love her. And I love Josie, because she's like the best crazy aunt a person could hope for."

That comment made Archie grin, the tension suddenly gone from his jaw. "Oh, I don't know," he said. "I had an honest-to-God crazy aunt. She was a concert pianist and traveled all over the world, but she didn't own a single piece of actual luggage. You'd always see her coming down the plane steps hauling paper bags full of her belongings. And she swore up and down that she'd only been married twice, even though the whole family knew she'd had three husbands."

I couldn't help smiling in response to his description. "She does sound like a crazy aunt. But Josie's mine, just like you're all part of this family we've created here in Globe. And that's why I gave Victoria the apartment. Because she's family to me, the same way you are, Archie."

He stood there, looking uncertain, and then reached over and gave me what was probably the world's quickest hug. And because he definitely wasn't the huggy type, I was so startled that I couldn't even react, only stood there like an idiot after he let me go, mumbling something about needing to dust the bookcases.

But that was all right. At least he understood now how much he and Victoria were loved, and how I'd always do whatever I could to make sure they were happy.

For some people, that might have been a small thing. For someone like Archie, who'd spent decades being very unhappy and who'd believed he might never be able to live a human life again, it was everything.

Now I just had to make sure he would continue to enjoy the life he'd built here in Globe.

Despite everything, I was feeling pretty upbeat as I left work that evening. True, I'd have to go home to an empty house—Calvin was working until nine—but it was still a house where I felt infinitely at home. Besides, I'd have Sadie to keep me company. She'd stayed at home that day because Calvin hadn't left for work until noon, but she was as thrilled to see me as though I'd been away for days and days.

After I walked her...and cranked up the A/C when I got back, because temperatures were still hovering just below the century mark...I poured myself half a glass of pinot grigio, figuring I'd put my feet up and read or watch TV for a while before I ventured into the kitchen to put together a salad or maybe nuke some leftovers, depending on how the mood struck me when the time came.

However, my cell phone rang just as I was about to reach for the remote control, and I instead leaned over to pick it up from where I'd left it on the coffee table.

Eddie Bixby.

Frowning a little, I accepted the call and put the phone to my ear. "Hi, Eddie. What's up?"

Because, although he'd texted me one more time after the competition to assure himself that I wasn't going to ask for my half of the winnings back, I hadn't heard from him since, and hadn't really expected to. He'd made a half-hearted effort to see whether I was interested in getting together to practice at some point, but I'd only told him I wasn't sure what I wanted to do next, so I needed to beg off for the time being.

"How are you?" he asked. "How's Archie?"

"I'm fine," I said, feeling increasingly puzzled. "Archie...well, I guess he's doing about as well as can be expected. How are you?"

"Fine," Eddie replied, but he sounded distracted, almost diffident. "Um...did you know about the competition that's coming up in the middle of July?"

I vaguely recalled there was another ballroom dance tournament being held in Tempe in a few weeks, but since I'd pretty much hung up my dance shoes, I hadn't been paying much attention. "Ye-es," I said, the syllable dragging out a little as I wondered again why he'd be asking me about it.

"Well, I—" He stopped there as he seemed to search for the right words. I could only hope he was a little more glib with the customers at the Toyota dealership where he worked. "I want to compete in it, and I wasn't sure where you and I stood with the whole dance thing, so I asked Joanna Greer if she'd like to be my partner going forward."

That revelation had definitely come from out of left field. I certainly didn't have any intention to keep competing, especially since my attempt to do some undercover investigating at the last tournament had turned out to be a big bust, but I had to admit his words surprised me a little.

"I thought Joanna was dancing with Tyler," I said.

"She was," Eddie replied. He sounded a little more relaxed now, as though he'd let out a relieved breath after realizing I wasn't going to give him grief for bailing out on me. "But that was just a temporary thing. And since I got the impression from you that you weren't sure you wanted to keep dancing, I reached out to her to see if she was interested in being my partner. Technically, I'm still in the novice category, but if I can place at the next competition after dancing with Joanna, then I can move up."

That sounded like a sensible enough plan to me. Eddie was a wonderful dancer, and he really needed to get out of the novice division.

"No, at the moment, I don't have any plans to compete again," I told him. "And I definitely don't want to leave you hanging. So I think it's great that Joanna wants to be your partner. You two are going to be fabulous together."

"You're sure?"

The relief in his voice was so palpable, I almost felt as though I could reach out and touch it over the airwaves.

"Totally sure," I said. "I had a great time

dancing with you, and it's wonderful that we did so well at Stepping Stars, but for me, it was more like fulfilling a bucket-list wish than anything I really want to keep doing."

Maybe just the slightest pause. Then Eddie said, "That's too bad. You're a really good dancer, and with some more practice, you could be great."

It was a good thing we were talking over the phone and not in person, or the flush that touched my cheeks at his compliment would have been awfully embarrassing. I'd meant what I said when I told him I wasn't interested in pursuing a career in professional ballroom dance, but at the same time, it was nice to hear I had some talents beyond reading Tarot cards or getting the odd flash of someone's aura.

Which still hadn't reappeared. I'd never really kept track, but I honestly couldn't remember the last time I'd gone this long in between seeing people's auras. Had the gift suddenly decided to desert me, for some reason?

I certainly hoped not. The auras could sometimes be intrusive and even a little startling, but that didn't mean I wanted them gone forever.

*Well, worry about it later,* I told myself. *Either they'll come back, or they won't. It's not as if you cast a spell to make them appear, so there isn't much you can do to compel them to return.*

This no-nonsense advice, if not exactly

welcome, at least allowed me to attend to the matter at hand.

"Thanks, Eddie," I said. "I appreciate that. But I think you and Joanna will do really well together. I'm sure the next time you go to the Stepping Stars competition, the two of you will blow everyone away."

He didn't deflect the compliment, but only replied, "That's what I'm hoping. She's an amazing dancer, and I know the judges really like her."

Considering that the judging staff was about seventy percent men who looked to be in their fifties or older, I didn't find that too surprising. I was firmly hetero, but even I could recognize Joanna's appeal. On the dance floor, she was absolutely spectacular.

"Well, I need to get back to work," Eddie said next. "I just wanted to check in with you and let you know what was going on so it wouldn't come as a complete surprise."

I was a little startled by his comment about having to get back to work—by that point, it was nearly six o'clock—but I realized a lot of car dealerships stayed open later so people would have a chance to go shopping after they were done working for the day. "No, I appreciate it," I told him. "And I wish you two the best of luck. Do you want me to go ahead and let Archie and Victoria know so they don't expect us for any more dance classes?"

"That would be great," Eddie said immediately, once again with that obvious note of relief in his voice. I could tell that was another call he hadn't been too eager to make. "Tell Archie he helped me a lot, and I'd be happy to give him a recommendation once he gets his studio up and running."

"I will," I promised. "You have a good evening, Eddie."

"You, too."

We ended the call there, and I set my phone back down on the coffee table. This development, while unexpected, made me feel a lot better about the situation. I wouldn't be ditching Eddie, and he'd get to dance with someone who was a much better match for him than I'd ever be. The only downside was that if I decided I needed to go undercover again, I'd have to find a new partner, but I didn't see that happening. My last attempt hadn't done me or Archie much good, so I doubted I'd give it another try.

No, there had to be some other way to solve this murder...even if I currently had no idea what that might turn out to be.

## 13

## Seeing Stars

THE NEXT WEEKEND WAS THE BIG FOURTH of July carnival in Globe. The actual holiday fell on a Tuesday, which meant an extra-long weekend for a lot of people, and a busy time at the shop. I had to admit I wasn't feeling much in the holiday mood —for the past few days, I'd been sort of off, even if I couldn't quite put my finger on the reason for the malaise that seemed to have settled over my mind and body like a murky fog. I told myself it was only because a month had now passed since Brad Masters was murdered, and I still wasn't any closer to tracking down the killer than I'd been when I started.

Which, I had to admit, was pretty frustrating. All of the other cases I'd been involved with had been solved in two weeks at the most, and now, as each day seemed to slip by a little faster, it felt as though we'd be up against Archie's trial date in no time. Yes, we still had more than six weeks to go, but....

Despite all those worries I couldn't quite shake, I made myself go to the carnival with Calvin and Archie and Victoria and Hazel and Chuck. Everyone did their best to act natural, and to studiously talk about subjects other than the trial that kept lurching ever closer, but I could still feel it looming over us, thick as the scent of kettle corn on the hot July air.

But I was glad the carnival appeared to be a raging success. The event brought in a lot of money for the town and for the high school's athletic department, and the throngs of people I saw around me that particular Sunday afternoon told me they'd probably have a record haul this year.

It was also a relief to see how no one seemed to pay any particular attention to Archie or, even worse, do their best to avoid him. True, he'd kept his regular hours at the store, and I hadn't seen any evidence to indicate my patrons were treating him any differently than they ever had, but this was a much larger group of people, and I'd been worried that he might have attracted some unwanted scrutiny by making such a public appearance at the carnival.

My worries seemed to be for nothing, though, and if he and Victoria had harbored their own fears about how the people attending the event might have reacted to his presence there, they definitely didn't show any sign of it. As far as I was able to tell, the two of them were forging ahead with their own plans, Victoria for the complete gut renovation of my apartment so she could turn it into a real office and showplace, and Archie for the dance studio he was determined to open, no matter what.

Setting up the studio had actually been a real piece of luck...or maybe the universe looking out for us in ways I hadn't expected. Al Torres, who'd owned the antique/junk store next door to Once in a Blue Moon for the past thirty-five years, had finally decided to retire. His kids had left Globe to pursue careers in Phoenix, so he didn't have anyone to leave his business to.

No, instead he'd ambled over to my store, gone up to Archie, who was working behind the cash register at the time, and said, "Heard you wanted to open a dance studio."

Because Archie wasn't the sort of person who surprised easily, he'd just gazed back at Al and replied, "Yes, I do."

"You can have my place," Al told him. "Lots of square footage on one level. Original wood floors. Interested?"

Of course Archie had been interested. He'd asked me if it was okay for him to go next door and have a look, and I'd told him to take as much time as he needed. After about ten minutes, he came back to the shop without Al and informed me, "I'm going to buy it. The place is perfect—and so is the price."

I didn't inquire as to how much Al was asking. That was none of my business, and something for Archie and Victoria to decide. But because I guessed that Al hadn't paid very much for his store-front back in the early eighties when he'd bought it, he'd decided to ask a fair market price but nothing too exorbitant.

Which was why the dance studio was currently in escrow...Archie had made it pretty clear that he didn't want me to step in with any financial help, even though I would have been happy to buy the place outright for him...and my two friends were acting like everything was on track and they had nothing to worry about.

Maybe that was their way of coping, of pretending the trial was no big deal. And I had to admit I was proud of them for not letting this bogus murder accusation get in the way of the future they wanted to share.

Problem was, if a jury didn't believe Archie was innocent, none of those careful plans would ever come to fruition.

"Want to go on the rollercoaster?" Calvin asked, bringing me back to the here and now.

It was a fairly small specimen, the sort of thing

that could be put up and taken down easily, nothing like the monsters I'd ridden at Six Flags back in California while I was in high school. All the same, looking at the coaster made my stomach do a queasy flip-flop.

Or maybe it was just the smell of all that hot grease floating on the air.

"No, I'm good," I said quickly. "But I can hang out here if the rest of you want to go ride it."

At once, Calvin shook his head. "It's fine. I can wait with you if everyone else wants to ride."

To my surprise, the rest of our companions—including Archie, who I was sure would have begged off—went ahead and got in line, while Calvin and I found a shadier place to stand and wait. It wasn't quite as hot as it had been in late June, since monsoon season had arrived right on schedule and the glaringly bright sun was shaded intermittently by big clouds floating by...a sign we might have some weather by the end of the day... but it was still way too hot to be standing out in the sun for any length of time.

Once we'd taken shelter under the overhang of a ball-toss game nearby, Calvin gave me a piercing look.

"Are you okay?"

"I'm fine," I said automatically. The scent of the hot grease was still making my stomach less than happy with me, but I had to admit I felt much better now that I was standing in the shade. "I guess it's just all kind of getting to me."

"The carnival?" Calvin asked, his gaze sweeping the crowded midway.

"No, all the stuff with Archie," I replied. "It feels like it's weighing on me more and more with every day that goes by. I've pulled cards and used my pendulum, and none of it seems to be doing any good."

He reached over and took my hand, the pressure of his fingers against mine infinitely reassuring. "Have you tried talking to your Grandma Ellen?"

Only my husband could comment so matter-of-factly about consulting the spirit of one's dead grandmother in a crystal ball. But then, my talks with her had been a part of my life ever since he and I had gotten together, so maybe his casual tone now wasn't so strange.

Unfortunately, Grandma Ellen was kind of a sore subject with me right then.

"I tried a few days ago," I said. "It took her a long time to appear, and when she did, she just told me that I already had all the information I needed and that she really couldn't interfere."

Calvin shook his head. "I'm sorry about that," he replied, then bent down to plant a soft kiss on the top of my head. "It does seem to be her standard line these days."

I couldn't even argue with his comment,

because it was the truth. Although Grandma Ellen had helped me in the past, it seemed like more and more the only thing she would say was that I needed to work these problems out on my own. Maybe she'd thought she was offering some reassurance by telling me I already had all the facts in hand and that I just needed to put the clues together, but those comments only made me feel worse about the situation. If the information I needed to lead me to the real killer really was within my grasp, why hadn't I figured it out?

*Because you're not as smart as you think you are,* I thought glumly, although I knew better than to say anything so self-deprecating out loud. Calvin seemed to have infinite belief in me and my abilities, and I knew he'd scold me...gently, but still...for doubting myself.

Archie and Victoria and Hazel and Chuck came over then, a little wind-blown from their ride on the rollercoaster, but looking cheerful and ready to move on to the next attraction.

"Let's see if we can win some stuffed animals," Hazel suggested after giving me a single sharp look, as though she'd realized we needed to do something next that didn't involve racketing around on tracks that probably should have been retired fifteen years ago.

I didn't know what I'd do with a stuffed animal even if I did manage to win one, but I still wanted to hug her for the suggestion. Trying to knock down some bottles or throw a bean bag through a hole in a painted backdrop seemed a lot more my speed.

And if either Calvin or I did manage to win something, well, we could donate the toys to a local charity. They always seemed to be looking for items like that to take to sick children in the hospital or to distribute at the local women's shelter, which generally took in families rather than women on their own.

Either way, playing the midway games would give me a chance to distract myself...and I knew I was sorely in need of some distraction right then.

---

Another week passed. I would have liked to say it was a peaceful one, but because Victoria's contractor had already started working on the remodel of the apartment upstairs, my workdays were filled with the sound of hammers, power tools, and heavy feet going to and fro. At least they were going to put off the reconstruction of the stairwell and the work on the new lobby at the rear of the building until the end of the project, meaning my break room remained untouched for the moment, but I still couldn't help wincing every time something particularly heavy was dropped on the floor above my head.

Archie, on the other hand, was on cloud nine —escrow had already closed on the antique store next door, and Al had handed over the keys and given his blessing. That meant my friend was spending most of his days in the place, walking through it with Brett, Josie's contractor nephew, who would be doing the majority of the work. It was much less involved than the remodel of my former apartment, because the dance studio mainly needed to have the floors sanded and refinished and a fresh coat of paint applied—well, along with a complete redo of the bathroom—meaning that Brett had been okay with taking it on. He was excellent at his job, but he was also severely overbooked, and had only taken the contract because he knew he could squeeze it in among his other projects.

However, when Archie came into work on Monday morning the next week, he looked as though he'd seen a ghost.

"Have you heard?" he demanded.

"Heard what?" I replied.

Looking annoyed, he pulled his phone out of his pocket. "This happened," he said, and thrust it toward me.

I took the phone from him and gazed down at the screen. I had to admit I hadn't been paying a lot of attention to what might be happening in the world at large lately, partly because I was wrapped up in everything that was going on in Globe, and partly because it just seemed safer to stay in my own little cocoon.

But as soon as I read the headline—"Second Ballroom Dancer Murdered at Local Event"—a rush of cold went through me.

It had happened again.

And that cold congealed into an awful lump in my stomach as I read further.

*Ballroom dance champion Edward Bixby was found murdered backstage at the Night of a Hundred Stars dance competition, held at the Westgate Hotel this past weekend. Police have not released any details of the crime, but eyewitnesses report that Mr. Bixby was also found in a trunk that belonged to one of the contestants, in an eerie echo of what happened to Brad Masters in late May.*

I looked up from the screen. My mouth was dry, and I had to fight to swallow against the painful lump in the back of my throat. "Someone killed Eddie?"

"It definitely looks that way," Archie said. He sounded curiously calm, although I supposed he'd had more time to process this awful information than I had. "You see what this means, though, don't you?"

About all I could do was send him a blank stare. "That the killer has struck again?"

His expression turned impatient. "Well, yes, of course. But beyond that, it means that now the police can't possibly believe I could be the killer. I was sixty miles away here in Globe when Eddie was murdered. And I was right here at the shop on Saturday morning, which is when it sounds as though his body was found. You were with me, obviously, and there are plenty of other people who can also corroborate my whereabouts."

Well, that was true. Saturday was always the busiest day at my store, meaning Archie had probably been seen working there by at least twenty or thirty people, maybe more. Also, Brett had stopped by the under-construction dance studio next door to get some odds and ends taken care of, and Archie had excused himself to go over and talk to him. That meant Brett could also be numbered among those who'd seen Archie in Globe that day.

As awful as I felt about Eddie and the terrible circumstances surrounding his death, I couldn't quite quell the rush of excitement that went through me as I thought of the implications of this new development. "Have you talked to your lawyer?"

"Yes," Archie said. "I called him as soon as I

saw the article. He told me he'd be in contact with Detective Murphy and the D.A.'s office, and would get back to me as soon as he could."

Of course Archie would be proactive about the situation. He'd want to get his name cleared as soon as possible so he could go on with his life.

But...poor Eddie. Not that anyone deserved to be killed in such a way, but he was a genuinely nice person, and utterly blameless.

Why had he been targeted, though? Had the murderer viewed him as a threat in some way?

That theory seemed pretty laughable. No, I hadn't known Eddie long enough for him to have revealed any deep, dark secrets to me, but he had the kind of open, sunny personality that seemed incapable of doing anything that would make him feel the need to hide it from others. At least Archie and Victoria could have been seen as some kind of competition to the killer, whereas Eddie had just partnered with Joanna Greer, and might not have been quite ready to head to the top of the open amateur division.

As soon as that thought went through my head, it was as if the universe had walked up to me and given me a wake-up slap to the face.

*Eddie had just partnered with Joanna Greer.*

Had we gotten the motive for these killings completely wrong? What if they had absolutely nothing to do with the competitions themselves, and everything to do with Joanna herself? What if someone was so obsessed with her, they were ready to kill anyone they saw as a potential rival?

I must have been looking positively gobs-macked, because Archie said impatiently, "What is it?"

"Something I just thought of," I replied. At that point, I wasn't sure whether I wanted to tell him about my latest theory about the killings, just in case I turned out to be completely off-base. Also, Archie had already reached out to his lawyer, who I knew must be in the process of contacting the Scottsdale D.A. and Detective Murphy. With that part of the procedure to exonerate my friend in the works, there wasn't much else I could do on our end...except talk to Joanna Greer and see if she could provide any information that might give me the clues I needed to find our killer.

And that meant I needed to track her down and hope she'd be willing to talk.

I remembered reading in the program from the Stepping Stars competition that she worked at a spa in Scottsdale, but it hadn't mentioned which one. Probably for the best, just because I doubted her clients would be too happy if some over-zealous fans showed up at her place of work so they could talk to her in person.

Then again, it wasn't too hard to track down that sort of thing on the internet.

It only took me a moment after typing in "Joanna Greer Scottsdale spa" to have the information pop up on my phone's screen. Yes, there was her name and photo on Sanctuary Wellness's website, along with her bio and credentials. No mention of her ballroom dance career, though, making me wonder whether she'd left out that information when she wrote up the biographical spiel, or whether the spa's owners had decided it was better to leave out that little piece of information about one of their aestheticians.

Not that it really mattered. What mattered was that I'd found her place of business, and that it was open today from eleven to eight. I supposed there was a possibility she wouldn't be working this afternoon at all, would be at home to recover from her grief over Eddie's murder, but I didn't think so. They hadn't been partners for very long, and although I knew next to nothing about her, I got the feeling she couldn't afford to blow off a day's work and annoy her clients just because tragedy had crossed her path for the second time in less than two months.

Still, better to check.

As Archie watched me, expression a combination of puzzlement and annoyance, I touched the screen to connect with the spa's office. The phone rang twice, and then a cheerful woman's voice said, "Sanctuary Wellness, how can I help you?"

"Is Joanna working today?" I asked. "I'd like to book a facial if she has any openings."

"Let me check," the receptionist said. If she'd heard anything on the news or online about what had happened to Joanna Greer's latest dance partner, it definitely didn't show in her voice. "Um, she had a cancellation, so she has room today at two. Will that work?"

While I would've liked to head right out the door in search of answers, I told myself two would work just fine. "That would be great," I said.

"Your name and number?"

I gave the receptionist both, figuring I'd been nothing more than a blip on Joanna's radar and that she probably wouldn't even remember who I was. After I thanked the woman and ended the call, Archie shot me one of his patented arched eyebrows.

"You're really going to drop everything in order to get a facial?"

"A facial with Joanna Greer," I responded, and comprehension immediately dawned in his expression.

"Do you think she's a suspect?" Archie asked, now sounding a little too eager.

"I don't think she's the killer, if that's what you mean," I said. "But I still want to talk to her and see what she knows."

That could have been impatience which flitted

across his features. Actually, I knew it was impatience. He could probably tell I wasn't giving him the whole story, and if there was one thing Archie hated, it was being left out of the loop. "Knows about what?"

"I don't want to say yet," I said. "Not until I have more corroborating evidence. But can you please watch the store after lunch?"

"Are you giving me a choice?"

"Not really," I said sweetly, and he released an exaggerated sigh.

"Then of course I can keep an eye on things while you're gone."

That was all he said, but I could tell he was looking forward to the day when the dance studio was open and he was his own boss and could set his own hours. Which was fine. I'd never expected his position at my store to last forever, and had mostly offered it to him so he'd have something to do with his time and as a way to explain how he was supporting himself. It made me happy to know that one day soon he'd spread his wings and go off on his own.

First, though, I had to see what Joanna knew about her stalker...or Archie might never be able to realize his dream.

## 14

## Stalk Dirty to Me

IT DIDN'T SEEM POSSIBLE THAT A PLACE could be hotter than Globe—the thermometer on my dashboard told me it was 101 degrees when I left town a little before one—but Scottsdale somehow managed it. As soon as I opened my Jeep's door, a wave of heat hit me, so strong that I felt lightheaded for a moment.

Amazing what a difference two thousand feet of altitude could make when it came to moderating Arizona's scorching summer heat.

I caught my breath and forced myself to climb out of the vehicle. At least I'd gotten lucky and had snagged a parking space near the spa's front entrance, so I wouldn't be forced to walk across miles of baking asphalt. It was so hot out there, I wouldn't have been surprised if one of my sandals stuck to the parking lot's surface.

Walking as fast as I could, I headed toward the door. It was an automatic one that whooshed open as I approached, letting out a welcome rush of cold air.

A woman probably a few years older than I sat at the receptionist's desk. She had perfectly high-lighted hair and long fuchsia-painted fingernails, and greeted me with, "Welcome to Sanctuary Wellness."

"Hi," I said. "I'm Selena. I have a two-clock appointment with Joanna."

The receptionist consulted her computer screen, then smiled. "We have the room set up for you. Come this way."

I followed her out of the reception area and down a hallway. The air conditioning had vanquished that moment of dizziness, and since the whole place had obviously been designed to be soothing—soft blue paint on the walls, Native American flute music playing quietly through unobtrusive built-in speakers—I felt myself relaxing just a little.

Not all the way, though. I wasn't here to unwind and get my pores opened, but to find out if Joanna knew anything about the murderer who'd apparently made her his target.

The receptionist showed me into a room with walls painted a much deeper color than those in the hallway, almost indigo. In contrast, all the furniture was white-finished wood and cream upholstery, making the space feel sleek and welcoming at the same time.

"You can sit down there, or on the table," she told me, gesturing toward one of a pair of chairs that had been placed in a corner. Yes, there was the usual massage table in the center of the space, waiting for me to lie down, but since I had no intention of actually getting a facial, the chair seemed a much more appealing alternative.

"Thank you," I replied, and went ahead and sat down on the closer of the two chairs.

She smiled at me, saying, "Joanna will be with you in just a moment. You can put on one of those robes there." And she pointed at a white robe hanging from a hook on one wall, then let herself out, closing the door behind her.

No need to wear a robe, since I wasn't really here for a facial. I pulled in a breath once I was alone, telling myself this was all going according to plan. The receptionist hadn't seemed suspicious at all, but then again, why would she? To her, I was just another client, and although I knew Joanna would probably recognize me the second she walked through the door—even though I knew I looked very different now, without the elaborate hair and makeup I'd worn at the competition—I had to hope she'd want to cooperate as soon as she understood my reason for being at her place of work.

Possibly, that was a far too optimistic view of the situation, but I was here now and therefore had to hope for the best.

A moment or two passed. Then the door opened, and Joanna came into the room. Like me, she looked a lot more casual than she had when competing, her bright red hair pulled back into a no-nonsense ponytail, her clothing a simple black tank top and black slacks, probably an ensemble required by the spa's management. Unlike me, she still wore heavy eyeliner and false eyelashes, although this set was a little less ostentatious than the rhinestone-accented ones she'd had on the last time I'd seen her.

As soon as she caught sight of me, those heavily lashed eyes narrowed. "You're Selena Marx," she said.

"Well, yes," I replied. "I figured you would have seen my name on your schedule."

"I did," she admitted, "but the name didn't ring a bell without a face to go along with it." She stopped there, as though wondering whether she should say anything else or whether she should just leave it alone. Obviously, she'd decided the situation required a few more questions, because she added, "What are you doing here?"

"I wanted to talk to you," I said simply. On the

drive over, I'd told myself I needed to be as honest with Joanna as possible. No, it wasn't in my nature to lie unless I absolutely couldn't avoid doing so, although I had to admit I'd dropped a fib here and there while in the middle of an investigation, telling myself it was all for the greater good.

In this case, though, I didn't suspect Joanna of being the killer, so there was no reason to dance around the issue with her. I just wanted to see if she had any information that might point me in the right direction, even if she might not realize a particular detail or tidbit could be the one thing that would crack the case wide open.

"About?" she returned, clearly not very happy with me. But before I could respond, she added, "And if you really just wanted to talk, you could have left me a message or something, instead of taking up my appointment time."

She sounded annoyed, and on that front, I couldn't really blame her. True, it had been a couple of years since I'd had to rely on my Tarot readings to pay the rent, but that time in my life wasn't so far back in the past that I couldn't remember what a pain it was to have people cancel on me, to make me go back and recalculate and see whether those missed appointments might mean I couldn't pay the electric bill on time.

"I'm going to pay you for the appointment," I told her, and I could tell from the shift in her posture that she'd immediately relaxed. "You don't need to worry about that. I wanted to talk to you about Eddie."

At once, her expression went still. "It was horrible," she said, tone flat, almost too expressionless. "But I've already talked to the police. I don't know anything about what happened. I was getting ready to go out on the dance floor when I heard someone scream. They'd—they'd found him, just like your friend Victoria found Brad."

The article Archie had shown me had already mentioned that particular fact, so this wasn't news to me. I supposed it shouldn't have been too surprising that the circumstances surrounding the discovery of Eddie's body were very close to what had happened when Victoria opened Archie's steamer trunk and saw Brad stuffed inside.

"I don't think you had anything to do with it," I said, and her posture relaxed a little bit more, although she still looked wary. "But I'm getting the feeling that someone is going after your partners, that they're being targeted, for whatever reason. That's the only connection between the two men, isn't it?"

Joanna hesitated for a moment. She glanced toward the closed door of the private room, as though worried that someone might be able to overhear what we were saying. I didn't find that very likely, since the door seemed sturdy enough and the music playing over the spa's sound system would most likely cover up anything going on inside the space we currently occupied.

Then she let out a breath, and came over and sat down in the empty chair next to mine. Her fingers—the nails expertly painted in a sort of modified French manicure, with the white tips replaced by an ombre shading of silver polish—rubbed against the knees of the sleek black pants she wore.

"I was thinking the same thing," she said, her voice low and tight. "I mean, I know it sounds crazy—like, I must have a pretty puffed-up ego to think I have some sort of crazy stalker, right?—but I couldn't think of a single reason why anyone would want to kill Eddie. He was one of the nicest guys I've ever met. Things were working out really well between us, and—"

She stopped there, and sent me a sideways look from under the heavy false eyelashes she wore. And even though she hadn't continued, I thought I'd gotten the idea.

Every instinct was telling me she and Eddie had been more than merely partners on the dance floor. No, they hadn't known each other for very long, but maybe that was just how Joanna operated. In order to be completely in sync with her companion on the dance floor, she needed to also do a completely different kind of dance with him in the bedroom.

Whatever worked, I supposed.

Her eyes were suspiciously bright now, and I could tell she was trying to hold back tears. Maybe Eddie had only recently come into her life, but it seemed to me that she'd cared for him quite a bit.

Too bad my ability to see auras seemed to have taken off for an extended vacation in the Bahamas. I really would have liked to get some visual confirmation of my suspicions.

"I'm so sorry," I said quietly. "Eddie was a wonderful person, and he definitely didn't deserve what happened to him. But that's why I have to ask —do you know anyone capable of doing something like this? Do you have any stalkers, any overzealous fans who might have been jealous?"

At once, she shook her head, even as her rose-glossed mouth twisted into a lopsided smile. "Not that I'm aware of. I mean, I guess I have some groupies—people who come to every competition, who ask for my autograph or whatever—but none of them have ever overstepped any lines. And yes, I get approached by men all the time who want to be my partner, but they back off when I tell them I already have a partner and aren't looking for anyone new to dance with. They're always respectful, not pushy at all."

I recalled the way Ron Whitman and Peter

Tillis had approached her at the mixer that one time, how she'd clearly given them the brush-off. "Maybe they act that way so they won't raise any suspicions," I suggested, and she gave a helpless lift of her shoulders.

"If that's really what's happening, then I don't know what to tell you. All I know is that I've been wracking my brains trying to think who would want to do something so horrible, and I can't come up with a single person who fits the bill." Joanna stopped there, her expression turning almost suspicious. "Why does it matter so much to you, anyway?"

"Because Archie Bradshaw is important to me," I replied at once. "I'm doing what I can to clear his name."

That didn't seem to be the answer she was looking for, since she still appeared dubious. "But he wasn't at the competition when Eddie was killed," she pointed out. "That means the cops will have to realize Archie wasn't responsible, right?"

"Well, that's our hope," I said frankly. "And Archie's lawyer is already reaching out to the D.A., hoping to get the charges dropped. But even with Archie off the hook, it seems to me we still need to discover who the real killer is. If he's targeting your dance partners on purpose, then that means anyone you try to dance with next will also be a target."

My ominous remark seemed to deflate her, because she slumped against the back of her seat and released another of those heavy breaths. "I know," she replied, now sounding defeated. "I've been thinking the same thing. Honestly, after what happened to Eddie, I'm not sure I'll even be able to find someone else who's willing to dance with me, and who could blame them? It's just...." The words trailed off, with a betraying tremble at the end. She seemed to gather herself, and went on, "It's just...I can't imagine not dancing. I'm only thirty—I'm not ready to hang up my dancing shoes yet, you know?"

I couldn't exactly know, because whatever drove her wasn't the same thing that drove me or made my life feel complete, but I thought I understood. There was something fun and wild and at the same time utterly controlled about that kind of dance, a kind of freedom you couldn't really experience anywhere else. I knew very little about Joanna Greer's life, but on the surface, it seemed fairly humdrum, routine. She needed that glamour and wildness and passion to make her world a better place.

A rush of anger went through me then, not just for the two men who'd lost their lives—Eddie especially—but for poor Joanna, who seemed to me another hapless victim of the violence perpetrated on her partners. All she'd wanted was to dance, and now, because some maniac had apparently made her the target of his unrequited desires, she might have to walk away from the one thing that made her happy.

"You won't have to," I said firmly, although I still had no idea how I was going to track down the killer. It was possible that the Scottsdale P.D.—and Detective Murphy in particular—had found more clues at the scene of this most recent crime, something that might point them in the right direction to find the culprit...but what if they hadn't? "I'll figure this out," I added, with more confidence than I felt.

Now Joanna looked totally skeptical. "How, exactly? Are you some sort of private detective or something?"

"'Or something,'" I agreed, holding back a smile. Although I didn't know her very well, it seemed fairly obvious to me that Joanna was a no-nonsense, down-to-earth type, and if I tried to explain I was a hedgewitch who relied on intuition, Tarot readings, pendulums—and the odd convo with my dead grandmother—to track down murderers, she'd probably laugh me right out of the room. "Let's just say that solving crimes is a hobby of mine. And I've solved about a half dozen so far, so I really do have a decent track record."

Her dubious expression didn't shift, although she didn't try to contradict me. "Well, I guess it's good you're trying to figure it out. Right now, I don't have a single clue as to who could be doing all this."

As she spoke, a faint line appeared between her eyebrows. Either she could add some serious acting chops to her resume in addition to her skills on the dance floor, or she was telling me nothing more than the truth.

Still, I wasn't quite ready to give up and abandon our interview. Maybe it was just that I'd driven all the way here and didn't want to face the prospect of returning to Globe without a single piece of helpful information...or maybe it was simply that I didn't feel like leaving the comfortable air-conditioned room and having to walk through that blast furnace of a parking lot to get back to my car.

"Maybe not a crazed fan," I said slowly. "But what about a jealous ex-boyfriend or someone like that?"

Although Joanna didn't shoot down that line of questioning right away, I could tell from the way her head tilted she was pretty sure I was on the wrong track.

"Brad was my boyfriend," she replied after the briefest of hesitations. "We were together for almost five years. Not that he was what you could call faithful the whole time."

Her tone sounded almost amused, something I

hadn't expected. Shouldn't she have been more upset that the man she'd spent nearly five years of her life with had cheated on her?

Before I could even begin to think of a neutral way to respond, however, she added, "And that's okay. Neither was I. We had what you could call an open relationship."

Well, that explained a few things, although I still thought she should have been more upset by Brad's death than she'd let on.

But people all grieved in their own ways, and I certainly wasn't here to police her reaction to his passing. However, her comment made another possibility occur to me.

"Even if it wasn't an ex-boyfriend of yours," I ventured, speaking slowly as I tried to work my way through the problem, "maybe it was one of Brad's other girlfriends, or one of those women's boyfriends?"

Joanna's lip curled ever so slightly. "Some of those 'girlfriends' were boyfriends," she said, now looking amused. "But I get what you're saying. I never met any of them, so I can't comment. However, most people who're in open relationships like that aren't really the jealous type. I can't see any of them killing Brad, let alone chopping him into little bits and hiding him in a steamer trunk."

Since I hadn't met any of the people in question, I'd have to take her word for it. But even if one of those girlfriends—or boyfriends—might have been capable of such an act of violence, it didn't take into account Eddie Bixby's death. There would have been no reason for any of them to murder him.

Which swung me right back around to Joanna. Every instinct I possessed was telling me she was the reason for these awful deaths, even if she couldn't think of anyone who might have done the deeds. All it meant was that the murderer was someone no one could ever have suspected.

And if that was the case, I didn't know how I could possibly figure out who they were. After all, Joanna was a lot closer to the situation than I was, and she appeared to be equally clueless.

"I get that you're trying to help," she said, and now her tone was softer, as though my disappointment had been written plain on my face for her to see. "And I honestly do appreciate it. But I've told the police everything I know, and I've lost hours of sleep trying to figure out who could be responsible. I think we're up against something that no one will be able to puzzle their way through. I mean, think of how many unsolved murders there are out there."

Now she sounded defeated, but I wasn't the type to give up so easily. I'd been in tighter places than this and had still managed to stumble my way to the solution of the mystery.

"I suppose that's true," I said. "But I'm going to keep trying. You don't mind, do you?"

Her lips pursed in what might have been the beginnings of a smile. "It's a free country."

Those words told me that, while she wouldn't stand in my way, neither would she do much to assist me going forward. Which was fine, because I really didn't see how she could be of any further help.

"Thanks," I said, then added, "How much do I owe you for the visit?"

No protest, just, "Let me write up a ticket for you."

Five minutes later, I was walking through the baking heat back to my Jeep, my main checking account $125 lighter. Not that I cared, except I really, really wished this interview had given me even the tiniest piece of information I could work with.

But it hadn't, and now I needed to get back to Globe.

Maybe once I was back on my home turf, I'd be struck by inspiration.

Right.

## 15

## Pregnant Pause

HOWEVER, ONCE I WAS BACK HOME—A quiet and empty home, since Calvin wouldn't get off work until six—I found myself just as flummoxed as I'd ever been. I'd petted Sadie and fed her a treat as a thank-you for being such a good dog while I was out, but the same questions kept haunting me.

Who had killed Brad Masters and Eddie Bixby...and why?

My head ached slightly, probably an after-effect from dealing with the Scottsdale heat. I turned the thermostat on the mini-split A/C unit that cooled the main parts of the house down to seventy, and went into the kitchen to pour myself a glass of iced tea. A few sips helped me feel a little better, and I wondered if I should grab a snack to tide me over until Calvin got home.

As soon as the thought went through my head, my stomach shifted uneasily. No, I couldn't call it exactly nausea, but the idea of eating anything felt extremely unappealing.

Okay, no snacks.

I took my glass of iced tea with me into my office, thinking I could try the Tarot and pendulum again, and see if the universe had decided to bestow any additional wisdom upon me now that I was sufficiently frustrated.

However, after I got out my Everyday Witch Tarot deck and shuffled it multiple times—and even lit some incense and passed the cards through the smoke so they'd be purified and ready to give me a true reading—I pulled the same three cards I had the first time I'd asked for assistance with this problem.

The Five of Wands, the Queen of Swords reversed, and the Magician.

For a long moment, I stood there in front of my desk, staring at the cards arrayed on the pretty cloth with its design of leaves and a many-rayed sun, the altar piece I always used during the summer months. It wasn't the first time I'd pulled duplicate cards when trying to get to the bottom of a question, and I realized the universe wasn't going to give me anything else to work with because it thought it had already provided me with the answers I required.

All right, time to bust out the pendulum.

But the pretty piece of carved fluorite would never land on a word or even a number, and kept stubbornly coming to a halt right between answers. This seemed to be a signal that the pendulum also thought I'd been given all the information I needed to work with, and therefore wasn't going to bother with a proper response.

Well, that was just great.

I expelled a sigh that sounded melodramatic even to me, and drank a few more swallows of iced tea. Maybe it was time to plop myself down on the couch in front of the TV and watch something mindless until Calvin came home, but on the other hand, I refused to give up so easily.

There was still something else I could try.

Another sip of iced tea to fortify me, and then I reached for the crystal ball that sat on one of my bookcases, placing the clear orb and the pretty carved stand it rested on right in the middle of my altar. True, the last time I'd reached out to Grandma Ellen, she'd been pretty cranky about the whole thing, and she might very well tell me this matter didn't concern either of us before disappearing in a puff of smoke...well, more like evaporating into a mist...but it would be doing Archie a disservice not to try. It might be that the deputy district attorney would decide to drop the case against him now it was clear he couldn't have murdered Eddie Bixby, and yet until I knew that for certain, I had to do everything in my power to clear my friend's name.

"Grandma Ellen," I said, and Sadie, who'd followed me into the office and settled herself in the little brown velvet bed I'd bought for her, pricked up her ears at the sound of my voice. "I need to talk to you."

The crystal remained stubbornly clear, but I wouldn't allow the utter lack of a response to deter me. Sometimes my grandmother appeared right away, and other times, it took her minutes to show up, as though she'd been off amusing herself on the astral plane and had to make her apologies to the other spirits who dwelled there before dropping into the crystal ball to see what I wanted.

"Grandma Ellen," I repeated, my tone now a little more pleading. "Please...it's important."

The faintest mist began to swirl inside the glassy depths, and I held my breath. Usually, that was a sign she was about to appear, but once or twice, I'd only seen the pale gray fog for a second or two before it evaporated, telling me I'd probably made contact but that she didn't want to be bothered at the moment.

This time, though, the mist began to grow more solid, and a few seconds later, my grandmother was staring back at me. As always, she looked the way she had when she was in her late thirties, pretty and fresh in appearance, with dark blonde hair and my same blue-gray eyes. Her mouth, coated in her favorite Cherries in the Snow lipstick, however, was pursed, telling me she wasn't terribly thrilled to be summoned this way.

"Another murder, I suppose," she said, in tones which seemed to indicate she knew that was the only reason I ever reached out to her these days.

"Two murders, actually," I replied. "The police suspect my friend Archie, but of course, he's innocent. I need to find out who the real killer is so Archie can be free to go on with his life."

A second or two passed as Grandma Ellen appeared to consider my request. Then she shook her head, the ends of her shoulder-length hair seeming to touch the inside of the crystal ball as she moved.

"How many times do I have to tell you that you already have all the information you need?" she asked.

About all I could do was shrug. "As many times as it takes for it to finally sink into my brain, I suppose," I responded. Luckily, I'd sounded more rueful than annoyed when I spoke, so I had to hope she wouldn't be too annoyed with me. "Can't you give me the teeniest hint?"

One eyebrow lifted. "I just did. It's unfortunate what happened to Archie, but you can figure this out, Selena—you always do."

*Thanks for the vote of confidence,* I thought, but I kept silent. I didn't want this to devolve into a bickering match.

No, I just wanted my Grandma Ellen to give me the information I so desperately needed.

"Was the murderer at the competition?" I asked, knowing even as I spoke how desperate the question must have sounded.

"Which competition?" she returned. "There were two, weren't there?"

That was the problem with communing with spirits...sometimes they could be entirely too literal.

"Either of them," I said, adding, "Or both."

She smiled a little. There was something knowing in that smile, as though she was in possession of knowledge I didn't currently have and was almost amused by it.

"Yes," she said. "The person you're looking for was there."

"At both events?" I persisted.

Her smile didn't waver. "You'll understand when you figure it out. For now, though, I think you need to pay more attention to yourself, rather than what's happening in the world at large."

What the heck was that remark supposed to mean? I took very good care of myself—made sure to eat right and get plenty of sleep, to meditate and do yoga at least four or five times a week. Why, I was probably one of the healthiest people in Globe.

"I'm fine," I told her. "But Archie may very well not be fine if I can't figure out who killed those two men."

Grandma Ellen's smile didn't even waver. "Possibly. I'm only saying there's something very important I think you've overlooked."

Before I could reply, fog swirled inside the crystal ball, and she disappeared. I had the sudden impulse to pick it up and shake it, hoping she might reemerge.

But it wasn't a Magic 8 ball, and I knew when my grandmother disappeared like that, she wasn't coming back any time soon. No, she'd delivered her message, and if I didn't have the brains to figure out what she was trying to say, well, that was on me.

I stood there for a moment, staring at the crystal, and then let out a breath and picked up the ball and its stand, and replaced them in their designated spot on the bookshelf.

Time to go watch some TV.

But I was never the type to sit idle for very long, and even as I tried to let myself get lost in the episode of *The Great British Baking Show* I'd selected, my brain wouldn't stop picking at Grandma Ellen's words, doing my best to decipher exactly what she was trying to say.

What had I overlooked? Did she know something about my health that she didn't want to tell me?

True, I'd had those few odd moments of queasiness, but it had been awfully hot lately, and even after living in Globe for more than two years, I still hadn't completely adjusted to Arizona's summer heat. I'd never gotten heat stroke or anything close to it, but there were a couple of times when I'd over-exerted myself during hot weather and ended up feeling a little dizzy.

This hadn't been dizziness, though.

Well, maybe it was getting close to that time of the month again. I hadn't been paying much attention lately, thanks to all the drama surrounding Brad Masters' murder and Archie's subsequent arrest, but I knew I was pretty well synced up with the full moon, which meant....

I stopped there, frowning. Which meant I should have had to deal with it over the long Fourth of July weekend, but it hadn't shown up.

Nor had it in June, when I'd been in the throes of getting ready for the replacement Stepping Stars competition with Eddie Bixby. I hadn't even thought about it, just because, once I'd had my

IUD put in some five years earlier, I skipped a month every now and again.

Except I'd had the IUD removed several months earlier. My doctor had told me things might be a bit irregular for a while, but....

My heart started to pound a little harder in my chest, even as I told myself the strange queasiness and other odd symptoms could be nothing more than stress.

Right. I'd never felt anything like this before, not even when Calvin was arrested for Dillon James' murder. If I hadn't reacted physically to all that anxiety back then, why would my body be acting like this now?

*I'm only saying that there's something very important I think you've overlooked.*

Did Grandma Ellen know something I didn't?

Well, that would be easy enough to find out.

I got up from the couch while Sadie looked at me with questioning eyes. But because she was curled up on her favorite pillow—she had beds all over the house but had decided that one particular pillow on the sofa worked just fine when she was in the living room—she didn't get up to follow me, only stayed where she was, chin resting on her front paws.

Trying to ignore the shaky feeling in my knees, I headed down the hall to the main bedroom and went into the *en suite* bathroom. Beneath the sink on my side of the double vanity I shared with Calvin was a stack of pregnancy tests. I'd bought them online because the two of us were trying to keep our attempts at getting pregnant on the down-low until we knew for certain that our little family was going to expand in the near future, and the last thing I wanted was for any of the clerks at the local Walmart or CVS to shoot me one of their all-knowing looks.

I got out one of the boxes, and then went through the slightly ignominious but necessary process of using the test. As I waited, I stared at myself in the mirror. I looked both pale and flushed, but that could have been because of the anxiety knotting in my stomach.

Or maybe there was a completely physical reason for the way I felt right then.

Those three minutes seemed interminable. Eventually, though, my watch told me the time was up, and I stared down at the little white stick I held.

Two very emphatic pink lines.

The world seemed to tilt under me, and I reached out with my free hand to grasp the edge of the quartz countertop so I wouldn't lose my balance. A hard blink, followed by another, was enough to bring me back to myself.

Calvin and I were going to have a baby.

A shudder went through my body, and I breathed in, then let it out. The two of us had been talking for months about this, about how much we wanted to have a child together, but it had never seemed real until the moment I looked down and saw those two pink lines staring up at me.

My first instinct was to grab my phone from my purse, now sitting on the dresser, so I could call Calvin and give him the good news. However, I really tried not to call him at work unless it was a dire emergency—most of his days as chief of the San Ramon Apache tribal police force were uneventful enough, but there were always exceptions to that rule, and he didn't need me reaching out over every little thing—and yet I thought this news was momentous enough that he'd want to hear it right away.

Almost at once, though, I dismissed that idea. This was probably the hugest news I would ever share with him...well, until we decided to try for Baby Number Two...and I wasn't sure I wanted to relay it over the phone. No, it would be much better if I told him in person. He'd be home in a couple of hours. Surely I could wait that long.

Determined upon that course of action, I wrapped up the pregnancy test in some tissue, then stowed it under the sink. The next two hours were going to feel interminable, I knew, but I figured I'd do what I always did when I needed to fill some time and keep myself from getting too antsy.

Feeling fluttery for an entirely different reason

than I had when I'd walked down the hallway a few minutes earlier, I made my way to the kitchen.

Because as this hedgewitch knew all too well, when you needed to kill some time, you might as well cook something.

---

"What's the occasion?" Calvin asked as he looked around the kitchen, at the pans strewn across the countertops and filling the sink, and the big pot of beef stroganoff simmering away on the stovetop.

"Um...I just felt like cooking," I replied. Now that he was here, looking very real and oh, so handsome in his uniform, I wasn't sure of the best way to break the news to him.

One eyebrow went up. That man knew me far too well. "I would have thought you'd be kind of tired after driving all the way out to Scottsdale and back."

He'd known where I was going because I'd texted him before I set out. It just seemed safer that way, in case I ended up having car trouble or getting stuck in traffic. "Oh, it wasn't too bad," I said, which was only the truth. I'd left Scottsdale before the afternoon rush hour really got up a full head of steam, so the drive had been more monotonous than anything else. "And I just thought it would be nice to put something together that we haven't had in a while."

"Fair enough." He came over and gave me a kiss, and a little thrill went through me at the touch of his lips on mine. Would I ever stop reacting to him like this?

Somehow, I doubted it.

"I'll go change, then come back and set the table," he said. "Then we can choose a wine for dinner."

I thought of all the drinks I'd had over the past month, how many times I'd carelessly consumed a glass of wine or a margarita. True, I hadn't known I was pregnant, but still, that behavior needed to stop now.

"Oh, I think I'll just have some water," I said hastily. "I still feel a little overheated from being in Scottsdale. But go ahead and pick out whatever you want to drink."

Now both his eyebrows lifted. It wasn't as though I went around consuming a bottle of wine by myself every day, but we usually had a glass with dinner during the week, sometimes a little more on a Friday or Saturday night if Calvin wasn't working the next morning.

All he said, though, was, "Well, maybe I'll skip it, too. Be back in a minute."

He disappeared down the hallway to the bedroom, and I drew in a breath. There might have been a moment during that exchange when I could have blurted out the news, but if there was, it had come and gone before I could recognize it.

Just as well. This was probably the sort of thing that would be better shared when we were both sitting down.

The egg noodles were done boiling, so I tipped them into a strainer and poured some lukewarm water over them, then transferred them to a bowl. The stroganoff itself went into another big serving bowl, and when I went to take the salad out to the table, it was to find Calvin already in the dining room, putting down placemats.

"Dinner's just about ready," I told him.

"That's fine. I'll be done with this in a minute."

I smiled, then went back into the kitchen to start bringing out bowls. Maybe it had been stupid to make something that put so much extra heat into the air, but I'd been hit with a sudden craving for stroganoff, and, since we had the ingredients on hand, had decided to go ahead and serve that for dinner.

Was this what the next nine months were going to be like? Would our meal planning depend entirely on what my hormones were telling me I wanted to consume any particular day?

I didn't know, but whatever happened, we'd just have to go along for the ride.

Well, unless that ride involved pickles and ice

cream or some other unholy combination. I had to draw the line somewhere.

The two of us sat down, while Sadie took up her usual position between the two of us, ready to consume any scraps we might throw her way. We tried to be careful about how much we fed her, since she was such a little thing, but we also knew there was no way in the world we could completely deny those big, begging brown eyes.

For a moment, Calvin and I were silent as we dished stroganoff and salad. Usually, if we were having wine, we'd kick off our meals with a little clink of our glasses together, but since water was on the menu tonight...and for the foreseeable future... there wasn't much to do except lift our tumblers and each of us help ourselves to an awkward swallow.

"So...how was the trip to Scottsdale?" he asked, after apparently gauging that I wasn't the one who wanted to initiate our dinner conversation. Honestly, my brain was so busy with trying to figure out how to break the news, I'd been sitting there silently, feeling more awkward than I should have been.

"Fine," I replied. "I mean, Joanna didn't have much to tell me, but just meeting with her made me think this whole thing is extremely personal. She said she doesn't have any stalkers, anyone who'd be so obsessed with her that they'd be willing to murder her partners, but I'm not so sure."

"Your intuition?"

Some men might have uttered those words in a mocking way, but I knew Calvin was only curious. By this point, he'd known me long enough to realize my gifts were real, even if they weren't always the most reliable things in the world.

Like those darn auras. I still couldn't figure out why they'd decided to take a powder these past few weeks.

"Yes," I said. "But I was feeling frustrated, so I reached out to Grandma Ellen."

Now Calvin looked almost surprised. He knew my grandmother had told me on several occasions that I should rely more on my own talents and pure gut instinct, and less on her. That I'd decided to contact her anyway only betrayed how frustrated I'd been feeling by the entire situation.

He was quiet, obviously waiting for me to go on.

Well, nothing for it.

I pulled in a breath, then said, "As usual, she told me I had all the facts already in hand. I'm not so sure about that, but it was pretty obvious she wasn't going to come out and tell me who killed Brad Masters and Eddie Bixby. There was something else, though, something she said I'd overlooked."

"A clue?"

"Not exactly," I replied. "This is more...personal." Despite the odd—or not so odd, now that I knew their source—bouts of queasiness I'd been suffering over the past couple of days, my stomach now seemed oddly quiescent, as if it knew it needed to leave me alone so I could tell Calvin this all-important news without being interrupted. "It's— Calvin, I'm pregnant."

For a second or two, he just stared at me, as if his brain hadn't quite made the leap from processing what it knew about the murder cases we'd just been discussing to something so much more personal. Then his face lit up, bright as the Arizona sun that still blazed down overhead, even though by then it was a little past seven o'clock in the evening.

"You're sure?" he asked, tone eager and yet just the tiniest bit hesitant at the same time, like that of a boy who'd been promised the latest Xbox but wasn't sure whether his parents were really on the level.

"Well, I only took the one test," I told him. "But it definitely had two of those bright pink lines."

At once, he plucked the napkin off his lap. "I want to see."

Not because he didn't trust me to be telling

him the truth, of course, but because he wanted to see such all-important evidence for himself.

Once a cop, always a cop, I supposed.

But since I'd anticipated his reaction and made sure to keep the little stick, I got up from the table and took him by the hand, then led him down the hall to our bedroom and into the attached bathroom. I bent down and retrieved the piece of plastic from where I'd stowed it under the sink, and handed it over.

Calvin stared down at it for a long moment. "It's real," he said, his voice barely more than a whisper.

"Yes," I replied, then took his hand again and gently removed the stick so I could set it down on the counter, and pressed his fingers against my still-flat belly. "We're going to be parents."

He stood there for a moment, palm firm against my stomach, dark eyes bright with excitement. But, since he was also the practical type, he said, "You'll need to make a doctor's appointment to be sure."

I'd already anticipated that kind of comment. "I know," I told him. "I'll call Dr. Carlisle in the morning. I'm sure she can squeeze me in somewhere."

That remark seemed to be the thing which truly sank in, even more so than the pregnancy test he'd been holding a moment earlier. "This is really happening," he said.

"It is," I agreed, and felt just the slightest flutter of unease. True, Calvin and I had been trying to get pregnant for the past few months, and I knew this was something we both wanted very much, but....

This might not be an ordinary pregnancy. As far as he knew, no one else in his shapeshifter tribe had ever had a child with someone who wasn't one of them. It might not matter in the least...or it could be a game-changer. Since we were treading unknown ground here, all we could do was hope everything would go smoothly.

And that I wouldn't have any symptoms that made my ob/gyn suspicious. Calvin had assured me that babies of the San Ramon tribe were born the regular way and his people's children didn't even begin to exhibit the coyote side of their natures until they were old enough to learn how to manage it, but....

But nothing. I wouldn't allow fear to take over. The universe had guided me to this moment, so I had to believe everything would be okay.

"Do you have any idea how much I love you?" Calvin asked, and I smiled.

"I may have a slight inkling," I teased him.

He bent down and kissed me on the lips, the caress both passionate and utterly, deeply tender.

"That's good," he said. "Because later tonight, I intend to show you exactly how much."

I thought of our dinner getting cold on the table, of a puzzled Sadie who'd slipped into her bed in the corner when we came into the master suite, wondering when we were actually going to eat.

Well, that's why microwaves had been invented.

I tilted my head up at my husband. "Why wait?" I asked, and pulled him toward the bed.

## 16

## Abracadaver

To my relief, Dr. Carlisle was able to slip me in at nine-thirty the next morning, since she'd had a cancellation. The timing worked out perfectly, because it meant I probably wouldn't be late for work and therefore wouldn't have to explain to Archie why I wasn't there to open the store. Not that he hadn't been the one to open up many times before, but any deviation in my schedule might raise questions. And although Calvin and I couldn't wait to make the big announcement, we also knew it was safer to hold off until I was past the all-important first trimester.

A physician's assistant took my vitals and drew some blood, then told me the doctor would be in to see me in just a couple of minutes. I glanced down at my watch, mostly to reassure myself time wasn't passing so quickly that I might be late to work, even though the office was only about five minutes from my shop and I'd be able to get there with plenty of time to spare.

True to the assistant's word, Dr. Carlisle entered the exam room about five minutes later. She was a trim woman in her early forties, with blonde hair always pulled back in a ponytail and attractive, no-nonsense features.

"It'll be a couple of days before we get the results back from the lab," she told me. "But you had a positive home pregnancy test?"

I nodded. "Two bright pink lines."

"Perfect," she said, and wrote something down on her clipboard. The office had plenty of modern equipment, but it appeared she liked to do patients' charts the old-fashioned way. "Date of your last period?"

I told her, and she made another note on her chart, looking pleased.

"That means you're probably about seven weeks along," she said. "But we'll wait for the results of the blood test to be sure. Once we have those in, then we can set up an appointment schedule, including an ultrasound."

"Is that usual?" I asked, hoping I didn't sound too alarmed at the prospect of getting that kind of test so early in my pregnancy.

The thing was, I'd never really expected to get married and settle down, let alone start a family. I wasn't one of those women who pored over *What to Expect When You're Expecting* and hung out in mom-to-be Facebook groups or whatever. This was all completely new territory for me, and therefore I really didn't know what was normal procedure and what was a sign that the doctor might be concerned about my health.

"It's fairly standard when you're over thirty and are having your first child," she said. "We just want to make sure everything is proceeding the usual way and we're not dealing with any surprises—not that I'm expecting any," the doctor added, probably in response to the expression of alarm I knew had just flitted across my face. "You're in excellent health, so I'm sure everything will be fine." She paused there before asking, "Is there anything else you want to know?"

Roughly ten thousand details or so, although I doubted Dr. Carlisle had time for that. "I know I should avoid alcohol and caffeine," I said, hoping I sounded cheerful about the prospect and not daunted by thoughts of not having my morning coffee or a glass of wine with dinner for at least the next year. "Anything else I should stay away from?"

She smiled. "Those recommendations change from week to week. My advice is to be moderate—eat healthy, get lots of sleep, drink plenty of water. You're probably fine having some green tea every once in a while, or a small piece of chocolate. Are you taking any supplements?"

"Just a multivitamin and some elderberry for immune health," I told her, and she nodded.

"You'll need to get on prenatal vitamins, but again, let's hold off on that until we get the results of the blood test. Once the pregnancy is confirmed, then I'll write you a prescription."

Making this all much more official. "That sounds good," I said. "I'll wait for your call."

"It should be sometime before the end of the day tomorrow," Dr. Carlisle told me.

That seemed like much longer to wait than I really wanted, but I knew the labs were busy and couldn't process a test instantly just because I was impatient.

*All good things to those who wait,* I told myself… and hoped the little aphorism was expressing nothing more than the truth.

"I'll wait to hear from you," I replied, then paused.

"What is it?" the doctor asked, her expression now amused. She'd probably seen that same questioning look on hundreds of patients' faces.

"Is it okay for me to keep working?" I said. "My job requires me to be on my feet a lot."

To my relief, she didn't appear overly concerned by that piece of news. "You'll be fine," she assured me. "Toward the end, you should probably try to get a stool or a chair to sit on, just to give your feet a break. But generally, it's good to stay active for as long as you can."

That was a welcome piece of news. Mentally, I'd already been preparing myself for the inevitable need to hire someone to come work at the store after Archie's dance studio was ready, but now that mission seemed even more urgent. Even if I was able to work at Once in a Blue Moon practically up until the moment when I went into labor, I still needed to make sure I had someone on board well before then so they could take over while I was at home with the baby. At the moment, I didn't have any plans to become purely a stay-at-home mom, but I realized I wanted to be there as much as I could for at least the first six months of my child's life, maybe longer.

So much to do, so much to plan for.

I thanked Dr. Carlisle, and once again she told me she'd be in touch just as soon as she heard back from the lab. After that, I headed out to my car and drove the quarter-mile or so to the shop, coming in the back door at five minutes until ten.

Because this part of the building was still untouched, everything looked normal. It didn't sound like business as usual, though, because once again the familiar hammering echoed down from upstairs, where the renovations on my former apartment were proceeding apace.

I hadn't seen Victoria's red Mercedes SUV, though, telling me she must be busy elsewhere, and the blue Beetle that had once been my car also wasn't in evidence.

However, Archie came in just a minute or so after I opened the cash register and started stocking it with that day's collection of coins and bills. He looked awfully cheerful for someone who had a cloud of suspicion hanging over his head, and I soon learned the reason why.

"The D.A. just called my lawyer," he said. "Apparently, the evidence is overwhelming that the same person committed both crimes, and since multiple witnesses informed them I was here in Globe when the second murder occurred, there's no way I could be responsible. They're dropping all charges."

Even though Archie wasn't exactly the huggy type, I couldn't help throwing my arms around him and giving him a squeeze. "That's wonderful news!" I exclaimed. "You must be so relieved."

He disentangled himself from the embrace, but carefully, as though to show me that, while he appreciated the gesture, he didn't want to prolong it any more than was strictly necessary. "I am relieved," he said calmly. "And so is Victoria."

"Where is she, anyway?" I asked. "I thought she'd be upstairs, overseeing the renovation."

Now looking pleased, Archie replied, "Oh, she

has a meeting with the builder's representative. They were very impressed by the work she did on our house when she showed it to them as an example of her design skills, and it sounds as though they're going to be signing a contract today."

I reflected that my friend had come a long way from his roots back in the 1950s. Somehow I doubted a man of that era would have been fine with allowing his fiancée to sign a contract without his input, but here was Archie, blithely letting Victoria handle the all-important piece of business on her own. True, I had a feeling she would have had some choice words for him if he'd tried to butt in, but still, I couldn't help thinking a lot of progress had been made.

"That's wonderful," I told him, thinking that my friend was just full of good news today. However, since I also guessed he wouldn't be too thrilled if I tried to hug him again, I just said, "It sounds as though everything is going your way."

"It does," he agreed. "And Brett let me know that he thinks the studio will be ready by the end of next week. Now that I don't have to worry about a murder trial, I want to start getting the word out. Do you think Hazel would be interested in doing any graphic design work for me?"

Good question. I knew she'd studied the subject in art school, although her first love was creating the gorgeous oil paintings that hung in several local galleries, or mural work, like the beautiful night sky scene she'd painted on the ceiling of my store. But she'd helped me out with flyers and other graphics projects as well, so I thought she might be game. Luckily, unlike his fraught relationship with Josie, Archie and Hazel got along just fine.

"You'd need to check what her schedule is like," I said. "I know she was working on a big piece that's going to a gallery in Gilbert, but I'm not sure when she's supposed to deliver it."

"I'll text her," Archie replied, telling me once again how many strides he'd made in adapting to life in the twenty-first century. A year ago, he hadn't even owned a cell phone...mostly because he was still a cat.

He went off to compose the text while I finished getting the store ready for opening. It was a Thursday, meaning I hoped we'd get more tourists passing through, even if the locals tended to reserve their shopping for the weekend.

"She's available," Archie announced a few minutes later. "We're going to meet this afternoon to discuss what I need." He paused there. "Do you mind if I leave a little early?"

"Not at all," I said, trying not to smile. He was so excited about his dance studio, and it wasn't as though I couldn't close up on my own. I'd done it hundreds of times before, after all.

The rest of the day was quiet enough, although late in the afternoon, I had to shoo out a couple of high school girls who apparently had decided their entertainment for the afternoon was smelling all the packets of incense and trying to figure out which ones they liked best. However, I still closed only a few minutes after five, and headed home just as soon as everything was locked up tight.

As I drove, I found myself wishing Calvin didn't have to work late tonight. Over dinner the day before—once we'd nuked everything in the microwave, since it was dead cold by the time we emerged from the bedroom—he'd told me he'd do his best to work it out with his deputies where he didn't have to be on shift during the evening once I was farther along in my pregnancy.

I'd been relieved, even as I'd known he wouldn't be able to settle on any adjustments to his schedule until we'd made the big announcement. And since that day was five weeks off in the future, I knew I'd just have to deal with the occasional evening alone until the proverbial cat was out of the bag.

At least I hadn't experienced any queasiness or moments of malaise while at work today. I chalked it up to being in a familiar environment surrounded by sights and scents that I loved...well, and also having an excellent HVAC system at the store.

Sadie had gone with me to work, so I wasn't greeted by an excited little dog. However, it was way too hot to take her on a walk yet—that would have to wait until the sun had dipped behind the mountains to the west—so I let her out in her dog run while I poured myself some herbal iced tea. Luckily, I loved herbal tea almost as much as I loved the caffeinated stuff, so drinking it wasn't exactly a hardship.

However, despite that welcome first sip of cool Lemon Mist, I found myself restless, not ready to sit down and relax. I didn't need to make dinner—my plan was to heat up some of yesterday's stroganoff—which meant I had a lot of idle time on my hands before Calvin came home a little after nine.

What to do with it, though? It wasn't as if I still had an overwhelming need to track down the person who'd killed Brad Masters and Eddie Bixby. Yes, what had happened was awful, but since Archie had been exonerated, it was time for me to step back and let the detectives at the Scottsdale P.D. do their work, right?

Definitely not right. No, Archie's future was no longer on the line, but didn't I owe it to Eddie to see if I could help in any way? Doing so wouldn't bring him back, and yet I had to believe the friends and family he'd left behind desperately needed that closure.

Problem was, I had no idea where to even start. Joanna hadn't given me any good leads, and Grandma Ellen's advice had been cryptic at best.

And yet....

Sadie scratched at the French doors that opened on the backyard, asking to come inside, even though she could have used the dog door. I headed over to open one of the doors for her, glass of iced tea in hand, and then let her in, a frown pulling at my brows.

Although my grandmother hadn't come out and said directly that the murderer had been in attendance at both events, she'd hinted that was the case.

Someone in the audience?

If so, I didn't know how I'd ever be able to track them down. It wasn't as though the organizers of the event would blithely turn over their credit card receipts for me to peruse, and even in the unlikely event that they might do so, who was to say the killer wasn't someone's plus-one or guest? In that case, there wouldn't be any record of them purchasing tickets...and that didn't even take into account a scenario where they might have paid cash.

There didn't seem to be much point in pursuing that particular avenue.

But there had also been all the dancers. None of them seemed like very likely suspects—from my limited time backstage at the Stepping Stars event, they all seemed preoccupied with their own hopes and fears—and yet I knew I couldn't ignore them, either.

After all, my grandmother had said I already possessed the information I needed to identify the killer.

Now I just needed to figure out how.

A sudden thought struck me, and I went into my office and over to the little magazine rack in the corner where I kept old issues of *Wicca* magazine, brochures from Globe's parks and recreation department, and anything else I wasn't quite ready to throw away but also didn't know what to do with.

Mixed in with the other ephemera were the programs from the two separate Stepping Stars tournaments.

I picked up both of them and took them with me out to the living room, along with my glass of iced tea. Sadie trotted along, mostly because she tended to follow me anywhere I went than because she thought food would be forthcoming any time soon. As soon as I'd seated myself on the couch, she jumped up and made herself comfortable on her favorite pillow.

Just having her there next to me made me feel a

bit better. It would be hours before Calvin got home, but at least I wasn't completely by myself.

I reached for the program from the first Stepping Stars competition, figuring I might as well go in chronological order. At the back, after the schedule of events and the inevitable advertising, were several pages that included head shots of all the participants, along with brief bios of each dancer. Both Archie's and Victoria's photos looked very professional, and I wondered when they'd had them done.

Everything was listed in alphabetical order, and I had to admit that by the time I got to Victoria's listing—under "P" for "Parrish"—I could feel my eyes beginning to glaze over. All those glamorous people seemed to have very ordinary lives, were real estate agents and dental hygienists, schoolteachers and IT professionals. Nothing about any of them seemed to stand out at all.

Until I got to Peter Tillis's entry.

*An auto restoration expert, Peter Tillis is a native of Phoenix and currently lives and works in Mesa. In addition to ballroom dance, he is also an accomplished amateur magician and can often be found performing at local clubs and private parties. Learn more about his magic at petertillis.com.*

For the longest moment, I sat stock still on the couch, staring down at the program. Instead of the printed words and the head shots arrayed on the page, though, a single image danced in front of my eyes.

The Magician card.

Who knew the Tarot could be so literal?

And now that the Magician's identity had snapped into place, the rest of it began to make a lot more sense. In this case, the Queen of Swords was Joanna, the object of Peter's desire. I'd noticed the way he was looking at her during the reception that followed the second Stepping Stars competition but had chalked it up to simple lust. There was no way in the world I could ever have imagined his need would drive him to do such terrible things.

The presence of the Five of Wands in the spread was a little murkier, although I guessed the Tarot had merely been trying to tell me how Peter's desire and jealousy had led him to a dark, conflicted place.

It all made a sort of horrible sense.

Problem was, I didn't have any idea as to what I should do now. I somehow doubted calling Detective Murphy and letting him know that the Tarot had told me Peter Tillis was the murderer would do much beyond getting me laughed right off the phone.

And while in the past I might have tracked

down Peter's place of work and confronted him directly, there was no way I'd do anything so crazy now. I was carrying Calvin's child, and that meant I needed to be careful.

Time to consult an expert.

I reached for my phone and entered my husband's cell number. He always carried the phone with him when he was on duty, so I knew he'd answer.

"Selena?" came his voice almost at once. "Is everything all right? Are you okay?"

"I'm fine," I said, knowing I needed to get the reassurances out of the way before I could move on to this latest revelation. "I'm sitting on the couch with Sadie and having a glass of Lemon Mist iced tea."

"Oh, okay," Calvin replied. "That's good. So...."

He let the syllable trail off, but I understood.

*So, why are you calling me at work?*

"I think I figured out who the murderer is," I said, and heard shocked silence on the other end of the line for a moment.

Then Calvin said, "Who is it?"

"A man named Peter Tillis," I said, knowing my husband probably wouldn't know Peter Tillis from the President of the United States. "He's another dancer, but in the novice division. He's an amateur magician but also, he's an auto restorer.

Could he have used a blowtorch or welding equipment or something like that to cauterize Brad Masters' wounds?"

"Probably," Calvin replied. His tone was calm, but I knew him well enough to detect the faint edge of excitement running underneath his words. "That kind of equipment would be powerful enough, and if he's an auto restorer, then he'd have easy access to it."

"I'm sure he's the killer," I said firmly. "But... what should I do now? I can't exactly go to Detective Murphy with something that's not much more than a hunch based on a Tarot reading."

My husband chuckled. "No, probably not. But you can call the Scottsdale P.D.'s tip line and say you have reason to believe Peter Tillis could be a person of interest because of his connection to the ballroom dance community and his access to welding equipment. Right now, they're probably feeling desperate enough that they'd follow up on that kind of tip."

"But what if they don't?" I asked then. Yes, Calvin's suggestion sounded like a reasonable enough one—and would keep me safely out of the line of fire—and yet I couldn't help worrying that Detective Murphy wouldn't think it was reason enough to drive over to Mesa to talk to Peter in person.

"Well, if that happens, then maybe I'll try to

talk to Detective Murphy directly," Calvin said. "For now, though, just call the tip line. It should be listed on the Scottsdale P.D.'s website."

Right. Maybe it wouldn't turn out to be enough, but, as my husband had just pointed out, we needed to take the first step.

"I will," I promised, then hesitated a second or two before saying, "Miss you."

"Miss you, too," he responded. "But I'll be home in just a couple more hours. Hang in there."

"Okay. Love you."

"Love you."

We ended the call there, but I didn't put down my phone. No, I opened a browser window, navigated to the Scottsdale police department's website, and then found the phone number for the tip line. It was a live link that dialed automatically, so after the recorded message had finished, I said clearly and slowly, "I have reason to believe Peter Tillis was involved in the murders of Brad Masters and Eddie Bixby. His access to welding equipment would have allowed him to cauterize their wounds, and he's an active member of the ballroom dance community."

Then I hung up.

Would it be enough?

I honestly didn't know.

## 17

## Bugging Out

NO ONE TRIED TO CALL ME BACK ABOUT the message I'd left on the tip line, and when Calvin got home, he just kissed me and said that, while the system probably had captured my phone number, there wouldn't have been any reason for an officer to reach out to me until they'd decided whether or not to follow up on the information I'd provided.

"You need to give it a couple of days," he told me, and while I understood these things took time, I couldn't help chafing at the delay. I hadn't been following what was going on in the ballroom dance world, but what if Joanna decided to acquire another partner after all, someone who might meet the same gruesome end?

I couldn't allow that to happen.

But because my husband had counseled patience, I did my best to do that very thing. I fell asleep in his arms that night, and got up the next morning, made breakfast, and prepped for work as though it was just an ordinary day with nothing special going on.

Of course, there was definitely nothing ordinary about getting a call from Dr. Carlisle around ten-thirty the next morning.

"We just got the test results," she told me. "You're definitely pregnant, and right at seven weeks along, just as I thought."

"Oh...wow," I replied, thinking even as I spoke how silly and inadequate those words were. Then I managed to gather myself and added, "So...what now?"

"We'll need to set up the ultrasound for around your tenth week," the doctor said. "And get all your appointments scheduled. I'll have my office manager contact you about that. Also, I'll call in the prescription for your prenatal vitamins. But otherwise—congratulations!"

"Thank you," I said.

She repeated that her office manager would be in touch, then ended the call. I stood there for a moment, staring down at my phone.

*Call Calvin,* my brain told me, but before I could touch the screen to connect the call, Archie emerged from the stockroom, where he'd been searching for incense packets to replace the ones that had been purchased the day before. Usually, it wouldn't have taken him so long, but we'd received several shipments over the past few weeks, and, what with everything else that had been going on in our worlds, we hadn't been as efficient with our inventory management as either of us would have liked.

He took one look at my face and immediately inquired, "What's wrong?"

"Nothing's wrong," I replied at once.

His eyebrow lifted. "Selena, you have the world's worst poker face. Something's going on. What is it?"

My resolution to keep quiet about my pregnancy had seemed a lot easier when I wasn't confronted by the all-too-real presence of one of my best friends staring me straight in the eyes and asking me what the matter was.

I hesitated for maybe all of five seconds. "Nothing's wrong," I said. "But if I tell you, this has to be between the two of us for now. You can't say anything to anyone, not even Victoria."

As soon as I made that demand, both his brows went shooting up. "For God's sake, Selena," he snapped. "How bad could it be?"

"It's not bad at all," I returned. "It's just... Calvin and I are pregnant."

Now it was Archie's turn to retreat into silence

for a few seconds. Maybe he was dumbfounded by my announcement, or maybe he was simply puzzling through that uniquely twenty-first-century turn of phrase, since back in his day, I doubted men were usually included in that sort of description.

Then again, it was entirely possible that his brain simply didn't want to acknowledge the sort of activities my husband and I would have had to engage in for me to be in my current condition.

Archie shifted his weight, asking, "You're sure?"

"Yes, I'm sure," I said calmly. "That was my doctor on the phone, letting me know she'd just gotten the lab results. I'm about seven weeks along, but I was waiting to say anything until I got past the first trimester. That's usually"—I broke off, hating to say the words but also knowing I had to face the reality of the situation—"that's usually when things go wrong. So now you know why I don't want to go spreading it all over town just yet."

"I completely understand," Archie replied, and I had no doubt that he did. Most likely, women had to confront that kind of devastating loss even more frequently back in his day. "And I won't say anything to anyone."

"Thank you," I said, and knew I could leave it

there. If Archie made a promise, he kept it. He might be crabby about the whole thing, but he would never go back on his word.

His expression turned almost solicitous. "Is there anything you need? Some water? Do you need to sit down?"

"I'm fine," I replied, doing my best to hold back a smile. "I feel great, and right now, there's absolutely no reason for me to change anything about my schedule or what I do while I'm here at the shop."

He nodded, but something about the look on his face told me he didn't entirely believe me. Since most TV shows made back in his day seemed to act as though babies were conveniently dropped off by a stork, I really didn't know what real-life women did in the 1940s and '50s when they were pregnant.

However, I somehow doubted they spent the entire nine months reclining on a chaise lounge, or whatever.

To my relief, though, he didn't argue, and only told me he was going to head over and start restocking the incense rack. That was fine by me, since it meant I could go to the crystal display and begin separating out the ones I wanted to put in the shop window next. I tried to rotate the arrangements in the window so they changed at least once a month, sometimes more than that if I was inspired...or simply looking for something to keep me busy.

As Archie was heading over to the counter, though, his phone buzzed in his pocket, and he reached in and pulled it out so he could glance down at the screen. Then he looked over at me and said, "Brett's next door and wants to have me look at the floor stain to make sure the color's what we discussed. Do you mind if I step out for a few minutes?"

"Not at all," I responded. "It's been quiet so far, and I doubt things are going to pick up until after lunch."

There was an understatement, considering we hadn't had a single customer set foot in the store so far this morning.

But Archie didn't contradict me, only uttered a quick thank-you and headed out. I continued to putter with the crystals, thinking it was time to shift out the red, white, and blue display I'd put in the window for the Fourth of July, and to instead create a tableau with warm, sunny colors like citrine and carnelian and topaz, something that could carry through the rest of the month and into August.

The bells on the shop door jingled, and I looked up, thinking Archie's consultation with Brett must have been awfully short. But then I froze, because I realized right away that wasn't Archie walking through the store's entrance.

No, it was Peter Tillis.

He looked a lot different from the last time I'd seen him, this time in jeans and work boots and a gray T-shirt.

Also, when we'd met at the mixer following the competition a few weeks ago, he hadn't been staring at me in murderous rage.

"You just couldn't keep your mouth shut, could you?" he growled, and my fingers tightened on the chunk of citrine I held.

Although I had a feeling it probably wouldn't do me any good, I still thought I should try acting dumb. "What the heck are you talking about?" I asked.

His eyes narrowed, as though he was gauging the distance between us and deciding whether he was close enough to make a lunge for me. Obviously not, since at least six feet and a table full of crystal specimens separated us.

"That call you made to the Scottsdale P.D.," he said. "A couple of their detectives paid me a little visit early this morning."

Well, at least that told me someone really had listened to my message and decided it had enough merit to send some detectives to talk to Peter. However, since he was now here in Globe rather than locked up, it seemed pretty obvious to me they'd decided he had enough of an alibi that they couldn't arrest him right away.

"How do you know I had anything to do with that?" I asked, and an unpleasant smile tugged at his thin lips.

"Because I know you went and talked to Joanna," he said. "I bugged the spa so I'd know exactly who was going in and out of there, who was talking to her."

"You bugged the *spa?*" I burst out. That was a whole level of obsession I hadn't even considered.

Peter's expression didn't shift. "I wanted to keep track of her. And I heard you talking about the murders, but since it seemed pretty obvious to me that you had no idea who the real killer was, I figured I'd leave it alone. But then you just had to call the tip line, and I realized you had to go. I worked too hard to make sure there was no way those murders could be traced back to me to have some crazy chick with a woo-woo store wreck the whole thing."

Anger flared at those disparaging words, although I told myself I had a lot more to worry about than a couple of ignorant insults. "You need to leave," I said calmly. "Coming here wasn't very smart. This is kind of a public place, in case you hadn't noticed."

"You sure about that?" Peter returned, now wearing an ugly sneer. "I mean, I've been watching your shop for the past hour, and you haven't had a single customer. And when Archie left to go next door, I figured I had the perfect opening."

Well, he had me there. Admittedly, the store hadn't been very busy this morning, and although Archie had made it sound as though his errand with Brett wouldn't take very long, I didn't know for sure how quickly he'd come back to the shop. He might have figured that, since business had been so slow today, he could hang around and chat for as long as he wanted.

I tried to reassure myself that even though Archie didn't have a lot of claims on his time this morning, I couldn't say the same for Brett. He'd need to get his business wrapped up so he could move on to the next project.

"Keep telling yourself that," I said. "Archie will be back any minute."

"That's all right," Peter replied. "This will only take a minute."

And he reached behind him and pulled a stubby-looking revolver out of the waistband of his pants, where presumably it had been hidden under the oversized T-shirt he wore.

This wasn't the first time I'd had a gun pointed at me, but it was the sort of experience that didn't exactly improve with repetition. Every cell in my body felt as though it had turned to ice, and my stomach made an uneasy flip-flop.

"Peter, you don't know what you're doing," I said, surprised my voice sounded so steady. "How many deaths do you want on your conscience? I'm pregnant."

His gaze flicked to my waistline, which of course hadn't begun to expand yet. Lip curling, he said, "You don't look pregnant."

"The doctor told me I'm seven weeks along."

For a second, he hesitated, the gun wavering just the slightest bit so it wasn't pointed straight at me, but more toward the rack of incense, which was located behind me and a little to the right.

I doubted I'd get a better opening than that.

Which was why I didn't even stop to think, but took the chunk of citrine I still held and hurled it at the hand that grasped the revolver.

It wasn't a direct hit, but the crystal did slam into his wrist. The gun went off, the sound shockingly loud in the enclosed space, even as I dropped to the floor.

Although I couldn't see exactly what had happened, I knew in the next instant that the bullet must have slammed into the incense display, because almost at once, the air was filled with the cloying aroma of packets of patchouli and sandalwood being released simultaneously. And just as I began to back away from the crystal table, thinking that maybe I could try scuttling on my hands and knees toward the back entrance like a crab running for cover, the bells on the shop door made a discordant jangle.

Archie and Brett burst into the store, took one look at Peter, who was already lifting the gun to get off another shot, and tackled him, sending him to the floor with an audible grunt as he fell behind another display table. From where I was crouched, I couldn't see exactly what happened next, but a moment later, Archie approached me, holding out a hand.

"Are you all right?" he asked, and I gave him a shaky nod, even as I pushed myself to my feet.

"I'm fine," I said. "He missed."

"I can see that," Archie said, his gaze moving to the mess of fine, aromatic dust that coated the incense display. He reached for his pocket, pulled out his phone, and said, "Mind if I call 9-1-1?"

"Not at all."

Now I could see that Brett was sitting on Peter, holding his arms behind his back in a tight hold I doubted was very comfortable. I mouthed a thank-you at him, thinking this wasn't the first time he'd come to my aid—and used his high school wrestling experience to help subdue a suspect—

even as I wondered how I could ever repay him for his timely intervention.

Not that he would accept any kind of reward. No, he'd just tell me he was glad he'd been in the right place at the right time once again.

Henry Lewis and several of his deputies showed up only a few minutes after Archie made his phone call, and soon enough, Peter was hauled off to cool his heels in the local jail. Now he was guilty of assault with a deadly weapon on top of everything else, and I had to wonder whose jurisdiction would have the first claim on him.

Well, that would be for the courts to decide, I supposed.

I was just glad that he'd probably be going away for a long, long time.

As it turned out, Peter was sent back to Scottsdale after the police searched his home and found bloodstains on one of his tailcoats, along with a cache of photos and videos of Joanna Greer that showed he'd been harboring his obsession for quite some time. She told Detective Murphy that Peter had actually approached her about being her partner on more than one occasion, and she'd shot him down in no uncertain terms every single time.

Whether those refusals were what had turned

him from an obsessed fan to a crazed killer, I didn't know. It would have been nice if she'd provided a little more information about those incidents when I went to talk to her, but it sounded as though she had enough unqualified dancers making similar appeals that she hadn't thought much about Peter's requests in particular.

And I remembered how he'd spoken to her at the mixer, although both of them had seemed pleasant enough during that encounter. If he'd been pressing his suit, Joanna hadn't shown any sign of it.

Peter sure wasn't talking, though. He'd refused his court-appointed attorney and apparently planned to defend himself when the case went to trial, which didn't seem like the wisest choice when you considered all the charges he was facing.

But now that the police had a solid suspect in jail, they revisited some of their interviews with other dancers who'd been backstage at the first Stepping Stars event, and who now remembered seeing Peter pass through while carrying several oversized duffle bags.

"I didn't think anything about it," one witness told them. "Everyone was always carting costumes and makeup kits and stuff like that around, so I just assumed that was what he had in the duffle bags."

It wasn't, of course. No, he'd been hauling the chopped-up pieces of Brad Masters first and Eddie

Bixby later on, both victims apparently murdered in the back of Peter's van and then moved into an available trunk backstage—after picking the locks, a talent that apparently was part of his magician's arsenal—so there wouldn't be any obvious way of tracing the remains back to him. Unless, of course, he allowed someone to see inside the vehicle, which I doubted would have ever happened.

And since Peter Tillis would soon stand trial for double homicide, I didn't know whether Henry Lewis would bother to pursue the separate case for assault. He was staying tight-lipped about the whole thing, probably waiting to see if Peter got a life sentence without the possibility of parole. If he received that sort of judgment for his original crimes, then there probably wasn't much reason to tack on another ten to fifteen years for coming after me with a gun.

No matter what happened, Peter's days as a free man were over.

And with that mess safely behind us, Calvin and I had invited all our closest friends over to the house for a barbecue. Monsoon storms threatened on that warm August evening, but I hoped they would hold off until we were done eating.

Everyone thought we were having our little get-together to celebrate the announcement that Peter Tillis's murder trial would take place in early October, but Calvin and I knew better. Dr. Carlisle had told me I was now in my second trimester, and so we'd decided it was time to share the happy news with our friends. I'd already called my mother and let her know, and Calvin and I had told his parents as well.

But this gathering was for all the other people we loved most.

So far, I wasn't showing very much, although I could tell the few pairs of jeans I owned were getting tight and would have to be abandoned fairly soon. All my sparkly skirts with their elastic waistbands would probably be good for another couple of months, however, and that was what I wore this evening.

My friend Hazel had shot a curious glance at the glass of Perrier I was holding, probably wondering why I wasn't drinking white wine or beer like everyone else, but to my relief, she hadn't asked any questions.

No, she waited until Calvin called out for everyone to gather around, saying we had an announcement we needed to make. They crowded close—Archie and Victoria and Josie and Hazel and Chuck—each one of them...well, except Archie...looking puzzled but game.

"We wanted you all here so we could tell you in person," I said, smiling at my gathered group of friends, thinking of how much my life had changed since I moved here a little more than two years earlier. "Calvin and I have some very happy news to share."

Now a knowing expression spread across Hazel's features, although she remained silent.

"We're going to have a baby," Calvin said. "Selena's due in mid-March."

Supposedly, a St. Patrick's Day baby, if all our calculations were correct, a dreamy little Pisces. Then again, first children often didn't arrive on schedule, so we might also have a fiery Aries, depending on when he or she decided to appear. After all, I was supposed to be a Cancer, a Moon Child—the reason why my mother had called me Selena—but I'd apparently had a different opinion on the subject, and had instead arrived two weeks early, on the summer solstice.

Not that it really mattered which day the baby was born. I'd love my child no matter which zodiac sign they were born under.

Everyone immediately erupted in various versions of well wishes for us and the baby, and our friends all gathered close, wanting to hug me and Calvin, or—in Archie's case—to shake his hand. It took a while for everything to settle down after that, but once we were seated and having some of my husband's excellent grilled tri-tip, the two of us exchanged a happy glance.

This was what we'd both hoped for—the start

of a new family, surrounded by the people who loved us and who we loved right back.

I couldn't ask for anything better than that.

*Selena's adventures continue in* Spell Check, *Book 10 in the Hedgewitch for Hire series.*

Also by Christine Pope

FAMILIAR SPIRITS

(Cozy Fantasy/Romance)

Spells and Spaniels

Cauldrons and Cats

Hexes and Hedgehogs

———

LATTES AND LEVITATION

(Cozy Mystery/Paranormal Romance)

Caffeine Before Curses

Muffins After Magic

Pastries and Prophecies

Eclairs and Ectoplasm

———

UNEXPECTED MAGIC*

(Urban Fantasy/Paranormal Romance)

Found Objects

Finders, Keepers

Lost and Found

Finding Destiny

---

## HEDGEWITCH FOR HIRE

(Cozy Mystery/Paranormal Romance)

Grave Mistake

Social Medium

Household Demons

Perpetual Potion

Jingle Spells

Wandering Monsters

Uninvited Ghosts

Prophet Motive

Ballroom Bits

---

## THE WITCHES OF WHEELER PARK*

(Paranormal Romance)

Storm Born

Thunder Road

Winds of Change

Mind Games

A Wheeler Park Christmas

Blood Ties

Healing Hands

Wishful Thinking

Smoke and Mirrors

---

MISS PRIMM'S ACADEMY FOR WAYWARD
WITCHES*

(Fantasy/Academy Romance)

Misspelled

Dispelled

Expelled

---

PROJECT DEMON HUNTERS*

(Paranormal Romance)

Unquiet Souls

Unbound Spirits

Unholy Ground

Unseen Voices

Unmarked Graves

Unbroken Vows

---

THE DEVIL YOU KNOW*

(Paranormal Romance)

Sympathy for the Devil

Charmed, I'm Sure

A Wing and a Prayer

Wish Upon a Star

---

THE WITCHES OF CANYON ROAD*

(Paranormal Romance)

Hidden Gifts

Darker Paths

Mysterious Ways

A Canyon Road Christmas

Demon Born

An Ill Wind

Higher Ground

Haunted Hearts

---

THE WITCHES OF CLEOPATRA HILL*

(Paranormal Romance)

Darkangel

Awoken

Illuminated

Stolen

Forgotten

Driven

Unspoken

---

THE WATCHERS TRILOGY*

(Paranormal Romance)

Falling Dark

Dead of Night

Rising Dawn

---

THE SEDONA FILES*

(Paranormal/Science Fiction Romance)

Bad Vibrations

Desert Hearts

Angel Fire

Star Crossed

Falling Angels

Enemy Mine

TALES OF THE LATTER KINGDOMS*

(Fantasy Romance)

All Fall Down

Dragon Rose

Binding Spell

Ashes of Roses

One Thousand Nights

Threads of Gold

The Wolf of Harrow Hall

Moon Dance

The Song of the Thrush

THE GAIAN CONSORTIUM SERIES*

(Science Fiction Romance)

Beast (free prequel novella)

Blood Will Tell

Breath of Life

The Gaia Gambit

The Mandala Maneuver

The Titan Trap

The Zhore Deception

The Refugee Ruse

---

STANDALONE TITLES

Hearts on Fire (Paranormal Romance)

Taking Dictation (Contemporary Romance)

Golden Heart (Gaslight Fantasy Romance)

Night Music: A Modern Reimagining of The Phantom
of the Opera (Contemporary Romance)

Ghost Dance: A Sequel to Gaston Leroux's The
Phantom of the Opera (Historical Mystery/Romance)

Flight Before Christmas (Fantasy Romance)

* Indicates a completed series

## About the Author

*USA Today* bestselling author Christine Pope has been writing stories ever since she commandeered her family's Smith-Corona typewriter back in grade school. Her work includes paranormal romance, cozy paranormal mystery, and urban fantasy, among others. She makes her home in beautiful Santa Fe, New Mexico.

*Christine Pope on the Web:*
www.christinepope.com

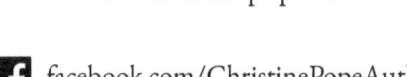 facebook.com/ChristinePopeAuthor

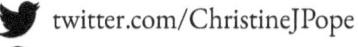 twitter.com/ChristineJPope

pinterest.com/ChristineJPope

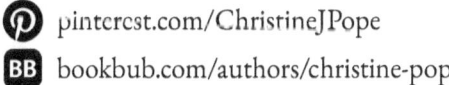 bookbub.com/authors/christine-pope